A SERIES OF UNFORTUNATE EVENTS

THE AUSTERE ACADEMY

Lemony Snicket

Illustrated by Brett Helquist

GALAXY

First published in Great Britain 2000
by
Egmont Books Ltd
This Large Print edition published by
BBC Audiobooks Ltd
by arrangement with
Egmont Children's Books Ltd
2004

ISBN 0 7540 7891 4

British Library Cataloguing in Publication Data

Snicket, Lemony
  The austere academy. —Large print ed.—(A series of
unfortunate events)
  1. Baudelaire family (Fictitious character)—Juvenile
fiction 2. Boarding schools—Juvenile fiction
  3. Orphans—Juvenile fiction 4. Children's stories
  5. Large type books
  I. Title II. Helquist, Brett
  813. 5'4[J]

ISBN 0-7540-7891-4

Printed and bound in Great Britain by
Antony Rowe Ltd., Chippenham, Wiltshire

For Beatrice—
You will always be in my heart,
in my mind,
and in your grave.

CHAPTER ONE

If you were going to give a gold medal to the least delightful person on Earth, you would have to give that medal to a person named Carmelita Spats, and if you didn't give it to her, Carmelita Spats was the sort of person who would snatch it from your hands anyway. Carmelita Spats was rude, she was violent, and she was filthy, and it is really a shame that I must describe her to you, because there are enough ghastly and distressing things in this story without even mentioning such an unpleasant person.

It is the Baudelaire orphans, thank goodness, who are the heroes of this story, not the dreadful Carmelita Spats, and if you wanted to give a gold medal to Violet, Klaus, and Sunny Baudelaire, it would be for survival in the face of adversity. Adversity is a word which here means 'trouble,' and there are very few people in this world who have had the sort of troubling adversity that follows these three children wherever they go. Their trouble began one day when they were relaxing at the beach and received the distressing news that their parents had been killed in a terrible fire, and so were sent to live with a distant relative named Count Olaf.

If you were going to give a gold medal to Count Olaf, you would have to lock it up someplace before the awarding ceremony, because Count Olaf was such a greedy and evil man that he would try to steal it beforehand. The Baudelaire orphans did not have a gold medal, but they did have an enormous fortune that their parents had left them, and it was that fortune Count Olaf tried to snatch. The three siblings survived living with Count Olaf, but just barely, and since then Olaf had followed them everywhere, usually accompanied by one or more of his sinister and ugly associates. No matter who was caring for the Baudelaires, Count Olaf was always right behind them, performing such dastardly deeds that I can scarcely list them all: kidnapping, murder, nasty phone calls, disguises, poison, hypnosis, and atrocious cooking are just some of the adversities the Baudelaire orphans survived at his hands. Even worse, Count Olaf had a bad habit of avoiding capture, so he was always sure to turn up again. It is truly awful that this keeps happening, but that is how the story goes.

I only tell you that the story goes this way because you are about to become acquainted with rude, violent, filthy Carmelita Spats, and if you can't stand reading about her, you had best put this book down and read something else, because it only gets worse from here. Before too long, Violet, Klaus, and Sunny Baudelaire will have so much adversity that being shoved aside by Carmelita Spats will look like a trip to the ice cream store.

'Get out of my way, you cakesniffers!' said a rude, violent, and filthy little girl, shoving the Baudelaire orphans aside as she dashed by. Violet, Klaus, and Sunny were too startled to answer. They were standing on a sidewalk made of bricks, which must have been very old because there was a great deal of dark moss oozing out from in between them. Surrounding the sidewalk was a vast brown lawn that looked like it had never been watered, and on the lawn were hundreds of children running in various directions. Occasionally someone would slip and fall to the ground, only to get back up and keep running. It looked exhausting and pointless, two things that should be avoided at all costs, but the Baudelaire orphans barely glanced at the other children, keeping their eyes on the mossy bricks below them.

Shyness is a curious thing, because, like quicksand, it can strike people at any time, and also, like quicksand, it usually makes its victims look down. This was to be the Baudelaires' first day at Prufrock Preparatory School, and all three siblings found that they would rather look at the oozing moss than at anything else.

'Have you dropped something?' Mr. Poe asked, coughing into a white handkerchief. One place the

4

Baudelaires certainly didn't want to look was at Mr. Poe, who was walking closely behind them. Mr. Poe was a banker who had been placed in charge of the Baudelaires' affairs following the terrible fire, and this had turned out to be a lousy idea. Mr. Poe meant well, but a jar of mustard probably also means well and would do a better job of keeping the Baudelaires out of danger. Violet, Klaus, and Sunny had long ago learned that the only thing they could count on from Mr. Poe was that he was always coughing.

'No,' Violet replied, 'we haven't dropped anything.' Violet was the oldest Baudelaire, and usually she was not shy at all. Violet liked to invent things, and one could often find her thinking hard about her latest invention, with her hair tied up in a ribbon to keep it out of her eyes. When her inventions were done, she liked to show them to people she knew, who were usually very impressed with her skill. Right now, as she looked down at the mossy bricks, she thought of a machine she could build that could

5

keep moss from growing on the sidewalk, but she felt too nervous to talk about it. What if none of the teachers, children, or administrative staff were interested in her inventions?

As if he were reading her thoughts, Klaus put a hand on Violet's shoulder, and she smiled at him. Klaus had known for all twelve of his years that his older sister found a hand on her shoulder comforting—as long as the hand was attached to an arm, of course. Normally Klaus would have said something comforting as well, but he was feeling as shy as his sister. Most of the time, Klaus could be found doing what he liked to do best, which was reading. Some mornings one could find him in bed with his glasses on because he had been reading so late that he was too tired to take them off. Klaus looked down at the sidewalk and remembered a book he had read called *Moss Mysteries*, but he felt too shy to bring it up. What if Prufrock Preparatory School had nothing good to read?

Sunny, the youngest Baudelaire,

looked up at her siblings, and Violet smiled and picked her up. This was easy to do because Sunny was a baby and only a little bit larger than a loaf of bread. Sunny was also too nervous to say anything, although it was often difficult to understand what she said when she did speak up. For instance, if Sunny had not been feeling so shy, she might have opened her mouth, revealing her four sharp teeth, and said 'Marimo!' which may have meant 'I hope there are plenty of things to bite at school, because biting things is one of my favorite things to do!'

'I know why you're all so quiet,' Mr. Poe said. 'It's because you're excited, and I don't blame you. I always wanted to go to boarding school when I was younger, but I never had the chance. I'm a little jealous of you, if you want to know the truth.'

The Baudelaires looked at one another. The fact that Prufrock Preparatory School was a boarding school was the part that made them feel the most nervous. If no one was interested in inventions, or there was nothing to read, or biting wasn't allowed, they were stuck there, not only all day but all night as well. The siblings wished that if Mr. Poe were really jealous of them he would attend Prufrock Preparatory School himself, and they could work at the bank.

'You're very lucky to be here,' Mr. Poe continued. 'I had to call more than four schools before I found one that could take all three of you at such short notice. Prufrock Prep—that's what they call it, as a sort of nickname—is a very fine academy. The teachers all have advanced degrees. The dormitory rooms are all finely furnished. And most important of all, there is an advanced computer system which will keep Count Olaf away from you. Vice Principal Nero told me that Count Olaf's complete description— everything from his one long eyebrow to the tattoo of an eye on his left ankle—has been programmed into the computer, so you three should be safe here for the next several years.'

'But how can a computer keep Count Olaf away?' Violet asked in a puzzled voice, still looking down at the ground.

'It's an *advanced* computer,' Mr. Poe said, as if the word 'advanced' were a proper explanation instead of a word meaning 'having attained advancement.' 'Don't worry your little heads about Count Olaf. Vice Principal Nero has promised me that he will keep a close eye on you. After all, a school as *advanced* as Prufrock Prep wouldn't allow people to simply run around loose.'

'Move, cakesniffers!' the rude, violent, and filthy little girl said as she dashed by them again.

'What does "cakesniffers" mean?' Violet murmured to Klaus, who had an enormous vocabulary from all his reading.

'I don't know,' Klaus admitted, 'but it doesn't sound very nice.'

'What a charming word that is,' Mr. Poe said. '*Cakesniffers.* I don't know what it means, but it reminds me of pastry. Oh well, here we are.' They had come to the end of the mossy brick sidewalk and stood in front of the

9

school. The Baudelaires looked up at their new home and gasped in surprise. Had they not been staring at the sidewalk the whole way across the lawn, they would have seen what the academy looked like, but perhaps it was best to delay looking at it for as long as possible. A person who designs buildings is called an architect, but in the case of Prufrock Prep a better term might be 'depressed architect.' The school was made up of several buildings, all made of smooth gray stone, and the buildings were grouped together in a sort of sloppy line. To get to the buildings, the Baudelaires had to walk beneath an immense stone arch casting a curved shadow on the lawn, like a rainbow in which all of the colors were gray or black. On the arch were the words 'PRUFROCK PREPARATORY SCHOOL' in enormous black letters, and then, in smaller letters, the motto of the school, 'Memento Mori.' But it was not the buildings or the arch that made the children gasp. It was how the buildings were shaped—rectangular,

10

but with a rounded top. A rectangle with a rounded top is a strange shape, and the orphans could only think of one thing with that shape. To the Baudelaires each building looked exactly like a gravestone.

'Rather odd architecture,' Mr. Poe commented. 'Each building looks like a thumb. In any case, you are to report to Vice Principal Nero's office immediately. It's on the ninth floor of the main building.'

'Aren't you coming with us, Mr. Poe?' Violet asked. Violet was fourteen, and she knew that fourteen was old enough to go to somebody's office by herself, but she felt nervous about walking into such a sinister-looking building without an adult nearby.

Mr. Poe coughed into his handkerchief and looked at his wristwatch at the same time. 'I'm afraid not,' he said when his coughing passed. 'The banking day has already begun. But I've talked over everything with Vice Principal Nero, and if there's any problem, remember you can always contact me or any of my associates at Mulctuary Money Management. Now, off you go. Have a wonderful time at Prufrock Prep.'

'I'm sure we will,' said Violet, sounding much braver than she felt. 'Thank you for everything, Mr. Poe.'

'Yes, thank you,' Klaus said, shaking the banker's hand.

'Terfunt,' Sunny said, which was her way of saying 'Thank you.'

'You're welcome, all of you,' Mr. Poe said. 'So long.' He nodded at all three Baudelaires, and Violet and Sunny watched him walk back down the mossy sidewalk, carefully avoiding the running children. But Klaus didn't watch him. Klaus was looking at the enormous arch over the academy.

'Maybe I don't know what "cakesniffer" means,' Klaus said, 'but I think I can translate our new school's motto.'

'It doesn't even look like it's in English,' Violet said, peering up at it.

'Racho,' Sunny agreed.

'It's not,' Klaus said. 'It's in Latin. Many mottoes are in Latin, for some

12

reason. I don't know very much Latin, but I do remember reading this phrase in a book about the Middle Ages. If it means what I think it means, it's certainly a strange motto.'

'What do you think it means?' Violet asked.

'If I'm not mistaken,' said Klaus, who was rarely mistaken, ' "Memento Mori" means "Remember you will die." '

'Remember you will die,' Violet repeated quietly, and the three siblings stepped closer to one another, as if they were very cold. Everybody will die, of course, sooner or later. Circus performers will die, and clarinet experts will die, and you and I will die, and there might be a person who lives on your block, right now, who is not looking both ways before he crosses the street and who will die in just a few seconds, all because of a bus. Everybody will die, but very few people want to be reminded of that fact. The children certainly did not want to remember that they would die, particularly as they walked beneath the arch over Prufrock Prep. The

Baudelaire orphans did not need to be reminded of this as they began their first day in the giant graveyard that was now their home.

CHAPTER TWO

As the Baudelaire orphans stood outside Vice Principal Nero's door, they were reminded of something their father said to them just a few months before he died. One evening, the Baudelaire parents had gone out to hear an orchestra play, and the three children had stayed by themselves in the family mansion. The Baudelaires had something of a routine on nights like this. First, Violet and Klaus would play a few games of checkers while Sunny ripped up some old newspapers, and then the three children would read in the library until they fell asleep on comfortable sofas. When their parents came home they would wake up the sleeping children, talk to them a little about the evening, and send them off to bed. But on this particular night, the Baudelaire parents came home early and the children were still up reading—or, in Sunny's case, looking at the pictures. The siblings' father stood in the doorway of the library and said something they never forgot. 'Children,' he said, 'there is no worse sound in the world than somebody who cannot play the violin who insists on doing so anyway.'

At the time, the Baudelaires had merely giggled, but as they listened outside the vice principal's door, they realized that their father had been absolutely right. When they first approached the heavy wooden door, it sounded like a small animal was having a temper tantrum. But as they listened more closely, the children realized it was somebody who cannot play the violin insisting on doing so anyway. The sounds shrieked and hissed and scratched and moaned and made other horrible sounds that are really impossible to describe, and finally Violet could take it no longer and

16

knocked on the door. She had to knock very hard and at length, in order to be heard over the atrocious violin recital going on inside, but at last the wooden door opened with a creak and there stood a tall man with a violin under his chin and an angry glare in his eyes.

'Who dares interrupt a genius when he is rehearsing?' he asked, in a voice so loud and booming that it was enough to make anyone shy all over again.

'The Baudelaires,' Klaus said quietly, looking at the floor. 'Mr. Poe said to come right to Vice Principal Nero's office.'

'*Mr. Poe said to come right to Vice Principal Nero's office*,' the man mimicked in a high, shrieky voice. 'Well, come in, come in, I don't have all afternoon.'

The children stepped into the office and got a better look at the man who had mocked them. He was dressed in a rumpled brown suit that had something sticky on its jacket, and he was wearing a tie decorated with pictures of snails. His nose was very small and very red,

17

as if somebody had stuck a cherry tomato in the middle of his splotchy face. He was almost completely bald, but he had four tufts of hair, which he had tied into little pigtails with some old rubber hands. The Baudelaires had never seen anybody who looked like him before and they weren't particularly interested in looking at him any further, but his office was so small and bare that it was difficult to look at anything else. There was a small metal desk with a small metal chair behind it and a small metal lamp to one side. The office had one window, decorated with curtains that matched the man's tie. The only other object in the room was a shiny computer, which sat in a corner of the room like a toad. The computer had a blank gray screen and several buttons as red as the pigtailed man's nose.

'Ladies and gentlemen,' the man announced in a loud voice, 'Vice Principal Nero!'

There was a pause, and the three children looked all around the tiny room, wondering where Nero had been hiding all this time. Then they looked back at the man with the pigtails, who was holding both hands up in the air, his violin and bow almost touching the ceiling, and they realized that the man he had just introduced so grandly was himself. Nero paused for a moment and looked down at the Baudelaires.

'It is traditional,' he said sternly, 'to applaud when a genius has been introduced.'

Just because something is traditional is no reason to do it, of course. Piracy, for example, is a tradition that has been carried on for hundreds of years, but that doesn't mean we should all attack ships and steal their gold. But Vice Principal Nero looked so ferocious that the children felt this was a time to honor tradition, so they began clapping their hands and didn't stop until Nero took several bows and sat down in his chair.

'Thank you very much, and welcome to Prufrock Preparatory School, *blah blah blah*,' he said, using the word 'blah' to mean that he was too bored to finish his sentence properly. 'I'm certainly doing Mr. Poe a favor in taking on three orphans at such short notice. He assured me that you won't cause any trouble, but I did a little research of my own. You've been sent to legal guardian after legal guardian, and adversity has always followed. "Adversity" means "trouble," by the way.'

'In our case,' Klaus said, not pointing out that he already knew what the word 'adversity' meant, ' "adversity" means *Count Olaf.* He was the cause of all the trouble with our guardians.'

'*He was the cause of all the trouble with our guardians,*' Nero said in his nasty, mimicking way. 'I'm not interested in your problems, quite frankly. I am a genius and have no time for anything other than playing the violin. It's depressing enough that I had to take this job as vice principal because not a single orchestra appreciates my genius. I'm not going to depress myself further by listening to the problems of three bratty children. Anyway, here at Prufrock Prep there'll be no blaming your own weaknesses on

20

this Count Olaf person. Look at this.'

Vice Principal Nero walked over to the computer and pressed two buttons over and over again. The screen lit up with a light green glow, as if it were seasick. 'This is an advanced computer,' Nero said. 'Mr. Poe gave me all the necessary information about the man you call Count Olaf, and I programmed it into the computer. See?' Nero pressed another button, and a small picture of Count Olaf appeared on the computer screen. 'Now that the advanced computer knows about him, you don't have to worry.'

'But how can a computer keep Count Olaf away?' Klaus asked. 'He could still show up and cause trouble, no matter what appears on a computer screen.'

'I shouldn't have bothered trying to explain this to you,' Vice Principal Nero said. 'There's no way uneducated people like yourself can understand a genius like me. Well, Prufrock Prep will take care of that. You'll get an education here if we have to break both your arms to do it. Speaking of which, I'd better show you around. Come here to the window.'

The Baudelaire orphans walked to the window and looked down at the brown lawn. From the ninth floor, all the children running around looked like tiny ants, and the sidewalk looked like a ribbon somebody had thrown away. Nero stood behind the siblings and pointed at things with his violin.

'Now, this building you're in is the administrative building. It is completely off-limits to students. Today is your first day, so I'll forgive you, but if I see you here again, you will not be allowed to use silverware at any of your meals. That gray building over there contains the classrooms. Violet, you will be studying with Mr. Remora in Room One, and Klaus, you will be studying with Mrs. Bass in Room Two. Can you remember that, Room One and Room Two? If you don't think you can remember, I have a felt-tipped marker, and I will write "Room One" and "Room Two" on your hands in permanent ink.'

'We can remember,' Violet said quickly. 'But which classroom is Sunny's?'

Vice Principal Nero drew himself up to his full height, which in his case was five feet, ten inches. 'Prufrock Preparatory School is a serious academy, not a nursery school. I told Mr. Poe that we would have room for the baby here, but we do not have a classroom for her. Sunny will be employed as my secretary.'

'Aregg?' Sunny asked incredulously. 'Incredulously' is a word which here means 'not being able to believe it,' and 'Aregg' is a word which here means 'What? I can't believe it.'

'But Sunny's a *baby*,' Klaus said. 'Babies aren't supposed to have jobs.'

'*Babies aren't supposed to have jobs*,' Nero mimicked again, and then continued. 'Well, babies aren't supposed to be at boarding schools, either,' Nero pointed out. 'Nobody can teach a baby anything, so she'll work for me. All she has to do is answer the phone and take care of paperwork. It's not very difficult, and it's an honor to

23

work for a genius, of course. Now, if either of you are late for class, or Sunny is late for work, your hands will be tied behind your back during meals. You'll have to lean down and eat your food like a dog. Of course, Sunny will always have her silverware taken away, because she will work in the administrative building, where she's not allowed.'

'That's not fair!' Violet cried.

'*That's not fair!*' the vice principal squealed back at her. 'The stone building over there contains the cafeteria. Meals are served promptly at breakfast time, lunchtime, and dinnertime. If you're late we take away your cups and glasses, and your beverages will be served to you in large puddles. That rectangular building over there, with the rounded top, is the auditorium. Every night I give a violin recital for six hours, and attendance is mandatory. The word "mandatory" means that if you don't show up, you have to buy me a large bag of candy and watch me eat it. The lawn serves as our sports facility. Our regular gym teacher, Miss Tench, accidentally fell out of a third-story window a few days ago, but we have a replacement, who should arrive shortly. In the meantime, I've instructed the children just to run around as fast as they can during gym time. I think that just about covers everything. Are there any questions?'

'Could anything be worse than this?' was the question Sunny had, but she was too well mannered to ask this. 'Are you kidding about all these incredibly cruel punishments and rules?' was the question Klaus thought of, but he already knew that the answer was no. Only Violet thought of a question that seemed useful to ask.

'I have a question, Vice Principal Nero,' she said. 'Where do we live?'

Nero's response was so predictable that the Baudelaire orphans could have said it along with this miserable administrator. *'Where do we live?'* he said in his high, mocking tone, but when he was done making fun of the children he decided to answer it. 'We have a magnificent dormitory here at Prufrock Prep,' he said. 'You can't miss it. It's a gray building, entirely made of stone and shaped like a big toe. Inside is a huge living room with a brick fireplace, a game room, and a large lending library. Every student has his or her own room, with a bowl of fresh fruit placed there every Wednesday. Doesn't that sound nice?'

'Yes, it does,' Klaus admitted.

'Keeb!' Sunny shrieked, which meant something along the lines of 'I like fruit!'

'I'm glad you think so,' Nero said, 'although you won't get to see much of the place. In order to live in the dormitory, you must have a permission slip with the signature of a parent or guardian. Your parents are dead, and Mr. Poe tells me that your guardians have either been killed or have fired you.'

'But surely Mr. Poe can sign our permission slip,' Violet said.

'He surely can *not*,' Nero replied. 'He is neither your parent nor your guardian. He is a banker who is in charge of your affairs.'

'But that's more or less the same

thing,' Klaus protested.

'*That's more or less the same thing*,' Nero mimicked. 'Perhaps after a few semesters at Prufrock Prep, you'll learn the difference between a parent and a banker. No, I'm afraid you'll have to live in a small shack, made entirely of tin. Inside there is no living room, no game room, and no lending library whatsoever. You three will each have your own bale of hay to sleep on, but no fruit. It's a dismal place, but Mr. Poe tells me that you've had a number of uncomfortable experiences, so I figured you'd be used to such things.'

'Couldn't you please make an exception?' Violet asked.

'I'm a *violinist*!' Nero cried. 'I have no time to make exceptions! I'm too busy practicing the violin. So if you will kindly leave my office, I can get back to work.'

Klaus opened his mouth to say something more, but when he looked at Nero, he knew that there was no use saying another word to such a stubborn man, and he glumly followed his sisters out of the vice principal's office. When the office door shut behind them, however, Vice Principal Nero said another word, and he said it three times. The three children listened to these three words that he said and knew for certain that he had not been sorry at all. For as soon as the Baudelaires left the office and Nero thought he was alone, he said to himself, 'Hee hee hee.'

Now, the vice principal of Prufrock Preparatory School did not actually say the syllables 'hee hee hee,' of course. Whenever you see the words 'hee hee hee' in a book, or 'ha ha ha,' or 'har har har,' or 'heh heh heh,' or even 'ho ho ho,' those words mean somebody was laughing. In this case, however, the words 'hee hee hee' cannot really describe what Vice Principal Nero's laugh sounded like. The laugh was squeaky, and it was wheezy, and it had a rough, crackly edge to it, as if Nero were eating tin cans as he laughed at the children. But most of all, the laugh sounded *cruel.* It is always cruel to laugh at people, of course, although sometimes if they are wearing an ugly hat it is hard to control yourself. But the Baudelaires were not wearing ugly hats. They were young children receiving bad news, and if Vice Principal Nero really had to laugh at them, he should have been able to control himself until the siblings were out of earshot. But Nero didn't care about controlling himself, and as the Baudelaire orphans listened to the laugh, they realized that what their father had said to them that night when he'd come home from the symphony was wrong. There *was* a worse sound in the world than somebody who cannot play the violin insisting on doing so anyway. The sound of an administrator laughing a squeaky, wheezy, rough, crackly, cruel laugh at children who have to live in a shack was much, much worse. So as I hide out here in this mountain cabin and write the words 'hee hee hee,' and you, wherever you are hiding out, read the words 'hee hee hee,' you should know that 'hee hee hee' stands for the worst sound the Baudelaires had ever heard.

CHAPTER THREE

The expression 'Making a mountain out of a molehill' simply means making a big deal out of something that is actually a small deal, and it is easy to see how this expression came about. Molehills are simply mounds of earth serving as condominiums for moles, and they have never caused anyone any harm except for maybe a stubbed toe if you were walking through the wilderness without any shoes on. Mountains, however, are very large mounds of earth and are constantly causing problems. They are very tall, and when people try to climb them they often fall off, or get lost and die of

starvation. Sometimes two countries fight over who really owns a mountain, and thousands of people have to go to war and come home grumpy or wounded. And, of course, mountains serve as homes to mountain goats and mountain lions, who enjoy attacking helpless picnickers and eating sandwiches or children. So when someone is making a mountain out of a molehill, they are pretending that something is as horrible as a war or a ruined picnic when it is really only as horrible as a stubbed toe.

When the Baudelaire orphans reached the shack where they were going to live, however, they realized that Vice Principal Nero hadn't been making a mountain out of a molehill at all when he had said that the shack was a dismal place. If anything, he had been making a molehill out of a mountain. It was true that the shack was tiny, as Nero had said, and made of tin, and it was true that there was no living room, no game room, and no lending library. It was true that there were three bales of hay instead of beds, and that there was absolutely no fresh fruit in sight. But Vice Principal Nero had left out a few details in his description, and it was these details that made the shack even worse. The first detail the Baudelaires noticed was that the shack was infested with small crabs, each one about the size of a matchbox, scurrying around the wooden floor with their tiny claws snapping in the air. As the children walked across the shack to sit glumly on one of the bales of hay, they were disappointed to learn that the crabs were territorial, a word which here means 'unhappy to see small children in their living quarters.' The crabs gathered around the children and began snapping their claws at them. Luckily, the crabs did not have very good aim, and luckily, their claws were so small that they probably wouldn't hurt any more than a good strong pinch, but even if they were more or less harmless they did not make for a good shack.

When the children reached the bale of hay and sat down, tucking their legs up under them to avoid the snapping crabs, they looked up at the ceiling and saw another detail Nero had neglected to mention. Some sort of fungus was growing on the ceiling, a fungus that was light tan and quite damp. Every few seconds, small drops of moisture would fall from the fungus with a *plop!* and the children had to duck to avoid getting light tan fungus juice on them. Like the small crabs, the *plop!*ing fungus did not appear to be very harmful, but also like the small crabs, the fungus made the shack even more uncomfortable than the vice principal had described it.

And lastly, as the children sat on the bale of hay with their legs tucked beneath them and ducked to avoid fungus juice, they saw one more harmless but unpleasant detail of the shack that was worse than Nero had led them to believe, and that was the color of the walls. Each tin wall was bright green, with tiny pink hearts painted here and there as if the shack were an enormous, tacky Valentine's Day card instead of a place to live, and the Baudelaires found that they would rather look at the bales of hay, or the small crabs on the floor, or even the light tan fungus on the ceiling than the ugly walls.

Overall, the shack was too miserable to serve as a storage space for old banana peels, let alone as a home for three young people, and I confess that if I had been told that it was my home I probably would have lain on the bales of hay and thrown a temper tantrum. But the Baudelaires had learned long ago that temper tantrums, however fun they may be to throw, rarely solve whatever problem is causing them. So after a long, miserable silence, the orphans tried to look at their situation in a more positive light.

'This isn't such a nice room,' Violet said finally, 'but if I put my mind to it, I bet I can invent something that can keep these crabs away from us.'

'And I'm going to read up on this light tan fungus,' Klaus said. 'Maybe the dormitory library has information on how to stop it from dripping.'

'Ivoser,' Sunny said, which meant

something like 'I bet I can use my four sharp teeth to scrape this paint away and make the walls a bit less ugly.'

Klaus gave his baby sister a little kiss on the top of her head. 'At least we get to go to school,' he pointed out. 'I've missed being in a real classroom.'

'Me too,' Violet agreed. 'And at least we'll meet some people our own age. We've only had the company of adults for quite some time.'

'Wonic,' Sunny said, which probably meant 'And learning secretarial skills is an exciting opportunity for me, although I should really be in nursery school instead.'

'That's true,' Klaus said. 'And who knows? Maybe the advanced computer really can keep Count Olaf away, and that's the most important thing of all.'

'You're right,' Violet said. 'Any room that doesn't have Count Olaf in it is good enough for me.'

'Olo,' Sunny said, which meant 'Even if it's ugly, damp, and filled with crabs.'

The children sighed and then sat quietly for a few moments. The shack was quiet, except for the snapping of tiny crab claws, the *plop!* of fungus, and the sighs of the Baudelaires as they looked at the ugly walls. Try as they might, the youngsters just couldn't make the shack into a molehill. No matter how much they thought of real classrooms, people their own age, or the exciting opportunity of secretarial skills, their new home seemed much, much worse than even the sorest of stubbed toes.

'Well,' Klaus said after a while, 'it feels like it's about lunchtime. Remember, if we're late they take away our cups and glasses, so we should probably get a move on.'

'Those rules are ridiculous,' Violet said, ducking to avoid a *plop!* 'Lunchtime isn't a specific time, so you can't be late for it. It's just a word that means "around lunch."'

'I know,' Klaus said, 'and the part about Sunny being punished for going to the administrative building, when she *has* to go there to be Nero's secretary, is completely absurd.'

'Kalc!' Sunny said, putting her little hand on her brother's knee. She meant something like 'Don't worry about it. I'm a baby, so I hardly ever use silverware. It doesn't matter that it'll be taken away from me.'

Ridiculous rules or not, the orphans did not want to be punished, so the three of them walked gingerly—the word 'gingerly' here means 'avoiding territorial crabs'—across the shack and out onto the brown lawn. Gym class must have been over, because all the running children were gone, and this only made the Baudelaires walk even more quickly to the cafeteria.

Several years before this story took place, when Violet was ten and Klaus was eight and Sunny was not even a fetus, the Baudelaire family went to a county fair in order to see a pig that their Uncle Elwyn had entered in a contest. The pig contest turned out to be a bit dull, but in the neighboring tent there was another contest that the family found quite interesting: the Biggest Lasagna Contest. The lasagna that won the blue ribbon had been baked by eleven nuns, and was as big and soft as a large mattress.

Perhaps because they were at such an impressionable age—the phrase 'impressionable age' here means 'ten and eight years old, respectively'— Violet and Klaus always remembered this lasagna, and they were sure they would never see another one anywhere near as big.

Violet and Klaus were wrong. When the Baudelaires entered the cafeteria, they found a lasagna waiting for them that was the size of a dance floor. It was sitting on top of an enormous trivet to keep it from burning the floor, and the person serving it was wearing a thick metal mask as protection, so that the children could only see their eyes peeking out from tiny eyeholes. The stunned Baudelaires got into a long line of children and waited their turn for the metal-masked person to scoop lasagna onto ugly plastic trays and hand it wordlessly to the children. After receiving their lasagna, the orphans walked further down the line and helped themselves to green salad, which was waiting for them in a bowl the size of a pickup truck. Next to the

38

salad was a mountain of garlic bread, and at the end of the line was another metal-masked person, handing out silverware to the students who had not been inside the administrative building.

The Baudelaires said 'thank you' to the person, who gave them a slow metallic nod in return. They took a long look around the crowded cafeteria. Hundreds of children had already received their lasagna and were sitting at long rectangular tables. The Baudelaires saw several other children who had undoubtedly been in the administrative building, because they had no silverware. They saw several more students who had their hands tied behind their backs as punishment for being late to class. And they saw several students who had a sad look on their faces, as if they had been forced to buy somebody a bag of candy and watch them eat it, and the orphans guessed that these students had failed to show up to one of Nero's six-hour concerts.

But it was none of these punishments that made the Baudelaire orphans pause for so long. It was the fact that they did not know where to sit. Cafeterias can be confusing places, because there are different rules for each one, and sometimes it is difficult to know where one should eat. Normally, the Baudelaires would simply eat with one of their friends, but their friends were far, far away from Prufrock Preparatory School, and Violet, Klaus, and Sunny gazed around the cafeteria full of strangers and thought they might never put down their ugly trays. Finally, they caught the eye of the girl they had seen on the lawn, who had called them such a strange name, and walked a few steps toward her.

Now, you and I know that this loathsome little girl was Carmelita Spats, but the Baudelaires had not been properly introduced to her and so did not realize just how loathsome she was, although as the orphans drew closer she gave them an instant education.

'Don't even *think* of eating around here, you cakesniffers!' Carmelita

Spats cried, and several of her rude, filthy, violent friends nodded in agreement. 'Nobody wants to have lunch with people who live in the Orphans Shack!'

'I'm terribly sorry,' Klaus said, although he wasn't terribly sorry at all. 'I didn't mean to disturb you.'

Carmelita, who had apparently never been to the administrative building, picked up her silverware and began to bang it on her tray in a rhythmic and irritating way. 'Cakesniffing orphans in the Orphans Shack! Cakesniffing orphans in the Orphans Shack!' she chanted, and to the Baudelaires' dismay, many other children joined right in. Like many other rude, violent, filthy people, Carmelita Spats had a bunch of friends who were always happy to help her torment people— probably to avoid being tormented themselves. In a few seconds, it seemed like the entire cafeteria was banging their silverware and chanting, 'Cakesniffing orphans in the Orphans Shack!' The three siblings stepped closer together, craning their necks to

41

see if there was any possible place to which they could escape and eat their lunch in peace.

'Oh, leave them alone, Carmelita!' a voice cried over the chanting. The Baudelaires turned around and saw a boy with very dark hair and very wide eyes. He looked a little older than Klaus and a little younger than Violet and had a dark green notebook tucked into the pocket of his thick wool sweater. *'You're* the cakesniffer, and nobody in their right mind would want to eat with you anyway. Come on,' the boy said, turning to the Baudelaires. 'There's room at our table.'

'Thank you very much,' Violet said in relief and followed the boy to a table that had plenty of room. He sat down next to a girl who looked absolutely identical to the boy. She looked about the same age, and also had very dark hair, very wide eyes, and a notebook tucked into the pocket of *her* thick wool sweater. The only difference seemed to be that the girl's notebook was pitch black. Seeing two people who look so much alike is a little bit eerie,

42

but it was better than looking at Carmelita Spats, so the Baudelaires sat down across from them and introduced themselves.

'I'm Violet Baudelaire,' said Violet Baudelaire, 'and this is my brother, Klaus, and our baby sister, Sunny.'

'It's nice to meet you,' said the boy. 'My name is Duncan Quagmire, and this is my sister, Isadora. And the girl who was yelling at you, I'm sorry to say, was Carmelita Spats.'

'She didn't seem very nice,' Klaus said.

'That is the understatement of the century,' Isadora said. 'Carmelita Spats is rude, filthy, and violent, and the less time you spend with her the happier you will be.'

'Read the Baudelaires the poem you wrote about her,' Duncan said to his sister.

'You write poetry?' Klaus asked. He had read a lot about poets but had never met one.

'Just a little bit,' Isadora said modestly. 'I write poems down in this notebook. It's an interest of mine.'

43

'Sappho!' Sunny shrieked, which meant something like 'I'd be very pleased to hear a poem of yours!'

Klaus explained to the Quagmires what Sunny meant, and Isadora smiled and opened her notebook. 'It's a very short poem,' she said. 'Only two rhyming lines.'

'That's called a couplet,' Klaus said. 'I learned that from a book of literary criticism.'

'Yes, I know,' Isadora said, and then read her poem, leaning forward so Carmelita Spats would not overhear:

*'I would rather eat a bowl of
  vampire bats
than spend an hour with Carmelita
  Spats.'*

The Baudelaires giggled and then covered their mouths so nobody would know they were laughing at Carmelita. 'That was great,' Klaus said. 'I like the part about the bowl of bats.'

'Thanks,' Isadora said. 'I would be interested in reading that book of literary criticism you told me about.

Would you let me borrow it?'

Klaus looked down. 'I can't,' he said. 'That book belonged to my father, and it was destroyed in a fire.'

The Quagmires looked at one another, and their eyes grew even wider. 'I'm very sorry to hear that,' Duncan said. 'My sister and I have been through a terrible fire, so we know what that's like. Did your father die in the fire?'

'Yes he did,' Klaus said, 'and my mother too.'

Isadora put down her fork, reached across the table, and patted Klaus on the hand. Normally this might have embarrassed Klaus a little bit, but under the circumstances it felt perfectly natural. 'I'm so sorry to hear that,' she said. 'Our parents died in a fire as well. It's awful to miss your parents so much, isn't it?'

'Bloni,' Sunny said, nodding.

'For a long time,' Duncan admitted, 'I was afraid of any kind of fire. I didn't even like to look at stoves.'

Violet smiled. 'We stayed with a woman for a while, our Aunt

45

Josephine, who was afraid of stoves. She was afraid that they might explode.'

'Explode!' Duncan said. 'Even I wasn't afraid as all that. Why aren't you staying with your Aunt Josephine now?'

Now it was Violet's turn to look down, and Duncan's turn to reach across the table and take her hand. 'She died too,' Violet said. 'To tell you the truth, Duncan, our lives have been very topsy-turvy for quite some time.'

'I'm very sorry to hear it,' Duncan said, 'and I wish I could tell you that things will get better here. But between Vice Principal Nero playing the violin, Carmelita Spats teasing us, and the dreadful Orphans Shack, Prufrock Prep is a pretty miserable place.'

'I think it's awful to call it the Orphans Shack,' Klaus said. 'It's a bad enough place without giving it an insulting nickname.'

'The nickname is more of Carmelita's handiwork, I'm sorry to say,' Isadora said. 'Duncan and I had to live there for three semesters because we needed a parent or guardian to sign our permission slip, and we didn't have one.'

'That's the same thing that happened to us!' Violet cried. 'And when we asked Nero to make an exception—'

'He said he was too busy practicing the violin,' Isadora said, nodding as she finished Violet's sentence. 'He always says that. Anyway, Carmelita called it the Orphans Shack when we were living there, and it looks like she's going to keep on doing it.'

'Well,' Violet sighed, 'Carmelita's nasty names are the least of our problems in the shack. How did you deal with the crabs when you lived there?'

Duncan let go of her hand to take his notebook out of his pocket. 'I use my notebook to take notes on things,' he explained. 'I plan to be a newspaper reporter when I get a little older and I figure it's good to start practicing. Here it is: notes on the crabs. They're afraid of loud noises, you see, so I have a list of things we did to scare them away from us.'

'Afraid of loud noises,' Violet repeated, and tied her hair up in a ribbon to keep it out of her eyes.

'When she ties her hair up like that,' Klaus explained to the Quagmires, 'it means she's thinking of an invention. My sister is quite an inventor.'

'How about noisy shoes?' Violet said suddenly. 'If we took small pieces of metal and glued them to our shoes? Then wherever we walked would make a loud noise, and I bet we'd hardly ever see those crabs.'

'Noisy shoes!' Duncan cried. 'Isadora and I lived in the Orphans Shack all that time and never thought of noisy shoes!' He took a pencil out of his pocket and wrote 'noisy shoes' in the dark green notebook, and then turned a page. 'I do have a list of fungus books that are in the school library, if you need help with that tan stuff on the ceiling.'

'Zatwal!' Sunny shrieked.

'We'd love to see the library,' Violet translated. 'It sure is lucky that we ran into you two twins.'

Duncan's and Isadora's faces fell, an expression which does not mean that the front part of their heads actually fell to the ground. It simply means that the two siblings suddenly looked very sad.

'What's wrong?' Klaus asked. 'Did we say something that upset you?'

'Twins,' Duncan said, so softly that the Baudelaires could barely hear him.

'You *are* twins, aren't you?' Violet asked. 'You look just alike.'

'We're triplets,' Isadora said sadly.

'I'm confused,' Violet said. 'Aren't triplets *three* people born at the same time?'

'We *were* three people born at the same time,' Isadora explained, 'but our brother, Quigley, died in the fire that killed our parents.'

'I'm very sorry to hear that,' Klaus said. 'Please forgive our calling you twins. We meant no disrespect to Quigley's memory.'

'Of course you didn't,' Duncan said, giving the Baudelaires a small smile. 'There's no way you could have known. Come on, if you're done with your lasagna we'll show you the library.'

'And maybe we can find some pieces of metal,' Isadora said, 'for noisy shoes.'

The Baudelaire orphans smiled, and the five of them bussed their trays and walked out of the cafeteria. The library turned out to be a very pleasant place, but it was not the comfortable chairs, the huge wooden bookshelves, or the hush of people reading that made the three siblings feel so good as they walked into the room. It is useless for me to tell you all about the brass lamps in the shapes of different fish, or the bright blue curtains that rippled like water as a breeze came in from the window, because although these were wonderful things they were not what made the three children smile. The Quagmire triplets were smiling, too, and although I have not researched the Quagmires nearly as much as I have the Baudelaires, I can say with reasonable accuracy that they were smiling for the same reason.

It is a relief, in hectic and frightening times, to find true friends, and it was this relief that all five children were feeling as the Quagmires gave the Baudelaires a tour of the Prufrock Library. Friends can make you feel that the world is smaller and less sneaky than it really is, because you know people who have similar experiences, a phrase which here means 'having lost family members in terrible fires and lived in the Orphans Shack.' As Duncan and Isadora whispered to Violet, Klaus, and Sunny, explaining how the library was organized, the Baudelaire children felt less and less distressed about their new circumstances, and by the time Duncan and Isadora were recommending their favorite books, the three siblings thought that perhaps their troubles were coming to an end at last. They were wrong about this, of course, but for the moment it didn't matter. The Baudelaire orphans had found friends, and as they stood in the library with the Quagmire triplets, the world felt smaller and safer than it had for a long, long time.

CHAPTER FOUR

If you have walked into a museum recently—whether you did so to attend an art exhibition or to escape from the police—you may have noticed a type of painting known as a triptych. A triptych has three panels, with something different painted on each of the panels. For instance, my friend Professor Reed made a triptych for me, and he painted fire on one panel, a typewriter on another, and the face of a beautiful, intelligent woman on the third. The triptych is entitled *What Happened to Beatrice* and I cannot look upon it without weeping.

I am a writer, and not a painter, but if I were to try and paint a triptych entitled *The Baudelaire Orphans' Miserable Experiences at Prufrock Prep*, I would paint Mr. Remora on one panel, Mrs. Bass on another, and a box of staples on the third, and the results would make me so sad that between the Beatrice triptych and the Baudelaire triptych I would scarcely stop weeping all day.

Mr. Remora was Violet's teacher, and he was so terrible that Violet thought that she'd almost rather stay in the Orphans Shack all morning and eat her meals with her hands tied behind her back rather than hurry to Room One and learn from such a wretched man. Mr. Remora had a dark and thick mustache, as if somebody had chopped off a gorilla's thumb and stuck it above Mr. Remora's lip, and also like a gorilla, Mr. Remora was constantly eating bananas. Bananas are a fairly delicious fruit and contain a healthy amount of potassium, but after watching Mr. Remora shove banana after banana into his mouth, dropping

53

banana peels on the floor and smearing banana pulp on his chin and in his mustache, Violet never wanted to see another banana again. In between bites of banana, Mr. Remora would tell stories, and the children would write the stories down in notebooks, and every so often there would be a test. The stories were very short, and there were a whole lot of them on every conceivable subject. 'One day I went to the store to purchase a carton of milk,' Mr. Remora would say, chewing on a banana. 'When I got home, I poured the milk into a glass and drank it. Then I watched television. The end.' Or: 'One afternoon a man named Edward got into a green truck and drove to a farm. The farm had geese and cows. The end.' Mr. Remora would tell story after story, and eat banana after banana, and it would get more and more difficult for Violet to pay attention. To make things better, Duncan sat next to Violet, and they would pass notes to one another on particularly boring days. But to make things worse, Carmelita Spats sat right behind Violet, and every few minutes she would lean forward and poke Violet with a stick she had found on the lawn. 'Orphan,' she would whisper and poke Violet with the stick, and Violet would lose her concentration and forget to write down some detail of Mr. Remora's latest story.

Across the hall in Room Two was Klaus's teacher Mrs. Bass, whose black hair was so long and messy that she also vaguely resembled a gorilla. Mrs. Bass was a poor teacher, a phrase which here does not mean 'a teacher who doesn't have a lot of money' but 'a teacher who is obsessed with the metric system.' The metric system, you probably know, is the system by which the majority of the world measures things. Just as it is perfectly all right to eat a banana or two, it is perfectly all right to be interested in measuring things. Klaus could remember a time, when he was about eight years old, when he had measured the width of all the doorways in the Baudelaire mansion when he was bored one rainy afternoon. But rain or shine, all

55

Mrs. Bass wanted to do was measure things and write down the measurements on the chalkboard. Each morning, she would walk into Room Two carrying a bag full of ordinary objects—a frying pan, a picture frame, the skeleton of a cat— and place an object on each student's desk. 'Measure!' Mrs. Bass would shout, and everybody would take out their rulers and measure whatever it was that their teacher had put on their desks. They would call out the measurements to Mrs. Bass, who would write them on the board and then have everybody switch objects. The class would continue on in this way for the entire morning, and Klaus would feel his eyes glaze over—the phrase 'glaze over' here means 'ache slightly out of boredom.' Across the room, Isadora Quagmire's eyes were glazing over too, and occasionally the two of them would look at one another and stick their tongues out as if to say, *Mrs. Bass is terribly boring, isn't she?*

But Sunny, instead of going into a classroom, had to work in the administrative building, and I must say that her situation was perhaps the worst in the entire triptych. As Vice Principal Nero's secretary, Sunny had numerous duties assigned to her that were simply impossible for a baby to perform. For instance, she was in charge of answering the telephone, but people who called Vice Principal Nero did not always know that 'Seltepia!' was Sunny's way of saying 'Good morning, this is Vice Principal Nero's office, how may I help you?' By the second day Nero was furious at her for confusing so many of his business associates. In addition, Sunny was in charge of typing, stapling, and mailing all of Vice Principal Nero's letters, which meant she had to work a typewriter, a stapler, and stamps, all of which were designed for adult use. Unlike many babies, Sunny had some experience in hard work—after all, she and her siblings had worked for some time at the Lucky Smells Lumbermill—but this equipment was simply inappropriate for such tiny fingers. Sunny could scarcely move the typewriter's keys, and even when she could she did not know how to spell most of the words Nero dictated. She had never used a stapler before, so she sometimes stapled her fingers by mistake, which hurt quite a bit. And occasionally one of the stamps would stick to her tongue and wouldn't come off.

In most schools, no matter how miserable, the students have a chance to recuperate during the weekend, when they can rest and play instead of attending wretched classes, and the Baudelaire orphans looked forward to taking a break from looking at bananas, rulers, and secretarial supplies. So they were quite distressed one Friday when the Quagmires informed them that Prufrock Prep did not have weekends. Saturday and Sunday were regular schooldays, supposedly in keeping with the school's motto. This rule did not really make any sense—it is, after all, just as easy to remember you will die when you are relaxing as when you are in school—but that was the way things were, so the

58

Baudelaires could never remember exactly what day it was, so repetitive was their schedule. So I am sorry to say that I cannot tell you what day it was when Sunny noticed that the staple supply was running low, but I can tell you that Nero informed her that because she had wasted so much time learning to be a secretary he would not buy any more when they ran out. Instead Sunny would have to make staples herself, out of some skinny metal rods Nero kept in a drawer.

'That's ridiculous!' Violet cried when Sunny told her of Nero's latest demand. It was after dinner, and the Baudelaire orphans were in the Orphans Shack with the Quagmire triplets, sprinkling salt at the ceiling. Violet had found some pieces of metal behind the cafeteria and had fashioned five pairs of noisy shoes: three for the Baudelaires and two for the Quagmires so the crabs wouldn't bother them when they visited the Orphans Shack. The problem of the tan fungus, however, was yet to be solved. With Duncan's help, Klaus had found a book on fungus in the library and had read that salt might make this particular fungus shrivel up. The Quagmires had distracted some of the masked cafeteria workers by dropping their trays on the ground, and while Nero yelled at them for making a mess, the Baudelaires had slipped three saltshakers into their pockets. Now, in the brief recess after dinner, the five children were sitting on bales of hay, trying to toss salt onto the fungus and talking about their day.

'It certainly is ridiculous,' Klaus agreed. 'It's silly enough that Sunny has to be a secretary, but making her own staples I've never heard of anything so unfair.'

'I think staples are made in factories,' Duncan said, pausing to flip through his green notebook to see if he had any notes on the matter. 'I don't think people have made staples by hand since the fifteenth century.'

'If you could snitch some of the skinny metal rods, Sunny,' Isadora said, 'we could all help make the staples after dinnertime. If five of us worked together, it would be much less trouble. And speaking of trouble, I'm working on a poem about Count Olaf, but I'm not sure I know words that are terrible enough to describe him.'

'And I imagine it's difficult to find words that rhyme with "Olaf,"' Violet said.

'It is difficult,' Isadora admitted. 'All I can think of so far is "pilaf," which is a kind of rice dish. And that's more a half-rhyme, anyway.'

'Maybe someday you'll be able to publish your poem about Count Olaf,' Klaus said, 'and everyone will know how horrible he is.'

'And I'll write a newspaper article all about him,' Duncan volunteered.

'I think I could build a printing press myself,' Violet said. 'Maybe when I come of age, I can use some of the Baudelaire fortune to buy the materials I would need.'

'Could we print books, too?' Klaus asked.

Violet smiled. She knew her brother was thinking of a whole library they could print for themselves. 'Books, too,' she said.

'The Baudelaire fortune?' Duncan asked. 'Did your parents leave behind a fortune, too? Our parents owned the famous Quagmire sapphires, which were unharmed in the fire. When we come of age, those precious jewels will belong to us. We could start our printing business together.'

'That's a wonderful idea!' Violet cried. 'We could call it Quagmire-Baudelaire Incorporated.'

'*We could call it Quagmire-Baudelaire Incorporated!*' The children were so surprised to hear the sneering voice of Vice Principal Nero that they dropped their saltshakers on the ground. Instantly, the tiny crabs in the Orphans Shack picked them up and scurried away with them before Nero could notice. 'I'm sorry to interrupt you in the middle of your important business meeting,' he said, although the youngsters could see that the vice principal wasn't sorry one bit. 'The new gym teacher has arrived, and he was interested in meeting our orphan population before my concert began.

Apparently orphans have excellent bone structure or something. Isn't that what you said, Coach Genghis?'

'Oh yes,' said a tall, skinny man, who stepped forward to reveal himself to the children. The man was wearing sweatpants and a sweatshirt, such as any gym teacher might wear. On his feet were some expensive-looking running shoes with very high tops, and around his neck was a shiny silver whistle. Wrapped around the top of his head was a length of cloth secured in place with a shiny red jewel. Such things are called turbans and are worn by some people for religious reasons, but Violet, Klaus, and Sunny took one look at this man and knew that he was wearing a turban for an entirely different reason.

'Oh yes,' the man said again. 'All orphans have perfect legs for running, and I couldn't wait to see what specimens were waiting for me here in the shack.'

'Children,' Nero said, 'get up off of your hay and say hello to Coach Genghis.'

'Hello, Coach Genghis,' Duncan said.

'Hello, Coach Genghis,' Isadora said.

The Quagmire triplets each shook Coach Genghis's bony hand and then turned and gave the Baudelaires a confused look. They were clearly surprised to see the three siblings still sitting on the hay and staring up at Coach Genghis rather than obeying Nero's orders. But had I been there in the Orphans Shack, I most certainly would not have been surprised, and I would bet *What Happened to Beatrice*, my prized triptych, that had you been there you would not have been surprised, either. Because you have probably guessed, as the Baudelaires guessed, why the man who was calling himself Coach Genghis was wearing a turban. A turban covers people's hair, which can alter their appearance quite a bit, and if the turban is arranged so that it hangs down rather low, as this one did, the folds of cloth can even cover the eyebrows—or in this case, eye*brow*— of the person wearing it. But it cannot cover someone's shiny, shiny eyes, or the greedy and sinister look that somebody might have in their eyes when the person looks down at three relatively helpless children.

What the man who called himself Coach Genghis had said about all orphans having perfect legs for running was utter nonsense, of course, but as the Baudelaires looked up at their new gym teacher, they wished that it weren't nonsense. As the man who called himself Coach Genghis looked back at them with his shiny, shiny eyes, the Baudelaire orphans wished more than anything that their legs could carry them far, far away from the man who was really Count Olaf.

CHAPTER FIVE

The expression 'following suit' is a curious one, because it has nothing to do with walking behind a matching set of clothing. If you follow suit, it means you do the same thing somebody else has just done. If all of your friends decided to jump off a bridge into the icy waters of an ocean or river, for instance, and you jumped in right after them, you would be following suit. You can see why following suit can be a dangerous thing to do, because you could end up drowning simply because somebody else thought of it first.

This is why, when Violet stood up from the hay and said, 'How do you do, Coach Genghis?' Klaus and Sunny were reluctant to follow suit. It was inconceivable to the younger Baudelaires that their sister had not recognized Count Olaf, and that she hadn't leaped to her feet and informed Vice Principal Nero what was going on. For a moment, Klaus and Sunny even considered that Violet had been hypnotized, as Klaus had been back when the Baudelaire orphans were living in Paltryville. But Violet's eyes did not look any wider than they did normally, nor did she say 'How do you do, Coach Genghis?' in the dazed tone of voice Klaus had used when he had been under hypnosis.

But although they were puzzled, the younger Baudelaires trusted their sister absolutely. She had managed to avoid marrying Count Olaf when it had seemed like it would be inevitable, a word which here means 'a lifetime of horror and woe.' She had made a lockpick when they'd needed one in a hurry, and had used her inventing skills to help them escape from some very hungry leeches. So even though they could not think what the reason was, Klaus and Sunny knew that Violet must have had a good reason to greet Count Olaf politely rather than reveal him instantly, and so, after a pause, they followed suit.

'How do you do, Coach Genghis?' Klaus said.

'Gefidio!' Sunny shrieked.

'It's a pleasure to meet you,' Coach Genghis said, and smirked. The Baudelaires could tell he thought he had fooled them completely and was very pleased with himself.

'What do you think, Coach Genghis?' Vice Principal Nero asked. 'Do any of these orphans have the legs you're looking for?'

Coach Genghis scratched his turban and looked down at the children as if they were an all-you-can-eat salad bar instead of five orphans. 'Oh yes,' he said in the wheezy voice the Baudelaires still heard in their nightmares. With his bony hands, he

68

pointed first at Violet, then at Klaus, and lastly at Sunny. 'These three children here are just what I'm looking for, all right. I have no use for these twins, however.'

'Neither do I,' Nero said, not bothering to point out that the Quagmires were triplets. He then looked at his watch. 'Well, it's time for my concert. Follow me to the auditorium, all of you, unless you are in the mood to buy me a bag of candy.'

The Baudelaire orphans hoped never to buy their vice principal a gift of any sort, let alone a bag of candy, which the children loved and hadn't eaten in a very long time, so they followed Nero out of the Orphans Shack and across the lawn to the auditorium. The Quagmires followed suit, staring up at the gravestone buildings, which looked even spookier in the moonlight.

'This evening,' Nero said, 'I will be playing a violin sonata I wrote myself. It only lasts about a half hour, but I will play it twelve times in a row.'

'Oh, good,' Coach Genghis said. 'If I

may say so, Vice Principal Nero, I am an enormous fan of your music. Your concerts were one of the main reasons I wanted to work here at Prufrock Prep.'

'Well, it's good to hear that,' Nero said. 'It's difficult to find people who appreciate me as the genius I am.'

'I know the feeling,' Coach Genghis said. 'I'm the finest gym teacher the world has ever seen, and yet there hasn't even been one parade in my honor.'

'Shocking,' Nero said, shaking his head.

The Baudelaires and the Quagmires, who were walking behind the adults, looked at one another in disgust at the braggy conversation they were overhearing, but they didn't dare speak to one another until they arrived at the auditorium, taking seats as far away as possible from Carmelita Spats and her loathsome friends.

There is one, and only one, advantage to somebody who cannot play the violin insisting on doing so anyway, and the advantage is that they often play so loudly that they cannot hear if the audience is having a conversation. It is extremely rude, of course, for an audience to talk during a concert performance, but when the performance is a wretched one, and lasts six hours, such rudeness can be forgiven. So it was that evening, for after introducing himself with a brief, braggy speech, Vice Principal Nero stood on the stage of the auditorium and began playing his sonata for the first time.

When you listen to a piece of classical music, it is often amusing to try and guess what inspired the composer to write those particular notes. Sometimes a composer will be inspired by nature and will write a symphony imitating the sounds of birds and trees. Other times a composer will be inspired by the city and will write a concerto imitating the sounds of traffic and sidewalks. In the case of this sonata, Nero had apparently been inspired by somebody beating up a cat, because the music was loud and screechy and made it quite easy to talk during the performance. As Nero sawed away at his violin, the students of Prufrock Prep began to talk amongst themselves. The Baudelaires even noticed Mr. Remora and Mrs. Bass, who were supposed to be figuring out which students owed Nero bags of candy, giggling and sharing a banana in the back row. Only Coach Genghis, who was sitting in the center of the very front row, seemed to be paying any attention to the music.

'Our new gym teacher looks creepy,' Isadora said.

'That's for sure,' Duncan agreed. 'It's that sneaky look in his eye.'

'That sneaky look,' Violet said, taking a sneaky look herself to make sure Coach Genghis wasn't listening in, 'is because he's not really Coach Genghis. He's not really any coach. He's Count Olaf in disguise.'

'I *knew* you recognized him!' Klaus said.

'Count Olaf?' Duncan said. 'How awful! How did he follow you here?'

'Stewak,' Sunny said glumly.

'My sister means something like "He

follows us everywhere,"' Violet explained, 'and she's right. But it doesn't matter how he found us. The point is that he's here and that he undoubtedly has a scheme to snatch our fortune.'

'But why did you pretend not to recognize him?' Klaus asked.

'Yes,' Isadora said. 'If you told Vice Principal Nero that he was really Count Olaf, then Nero could throw the cakesniffer out of here, if you'll pardon my language.'

Violet shook her head to indicate that she disagreed with Isadora and that she didn't mind about 'cakesniffer.' 'Olaf's too clever for that,' she said. 'I knew that if I tried to tell Nero that he wasn't really a gym teacher, he would manage to wiggle out of it, just as he did with Aunt Josephine and Uncle Monty and everybody else.'

'That's good thinking,' Klaus admitted. 'Plus, if Olaf thinks that he's fooled us, it might give us some more time to figure out exactly what he's up to.'

'Lirt!' Sunny pointed out.

'My sister means that we can see if any of his assistants are around,' Violet translated. 'That's a good point, Sunny. I hadn't thought of that.'

'Count Olaf has assistants?' Isadora asked. 'That's not fair. He's bad enough without people helping him.'

'His assistants are as bad as he is,' Klaus said. 'There are two powder-faced women who forced us to be in his play. There's a hook-handed man who helped Olaf murder our Uncle Monty.'

'And the bald man who bossed us around at the lumbermill, don't forget him,' Violet added.

'Aeginu!' Sunny said, which meant something like 'And the assistant that looks like neither a man nor a woman.'

'What does "aeginu" mean?' Duncan asked, taking out his notebook. 'I'm going to write down all these details about Olaf and his troupe.'

'Why?' Violet asked.

'Why?' Isadora repeated. 'Because we're going to help you, that's why! You don't think we'd just sit here while you tried to escape from Olaf's clutches, would you?'

'But Count Olaf is very dangerous,' Klaus said. 'If you try and help us, you'll be risking your lives.'

'Never mind about that,' Duncan said, although I am sorry to tell you that the Quagmire triplets should have minded about that. They should have minded very much. Duncan and Isadora were very brave and caring to try and help the Baudelaire orphans, but bravery often demands a price. By 'price' I do not mean something along the lines of five dollars. I mean a much, much bigger price, a price so dreadful that I cannot speak of it now but must return to the scene I am writing at this moment.

'Never mind about that,' Duncan said. 'What we need is a plan. Now, we need to prove to Nero that Coach Genghis is really Count Olaf. How can we do that?'

'Nero has that computer,' Violet said thoughtfully. 'He showed us a little picture of Olaf on the screen, remember?'

'Yes,' Klaus said, shaking his head.

'He told us that the advanced computer system would keep Olaf away. So much for computers.'

Sunny nodded her head in agreement, and Violet picked her up and put her on her lap. Nero had reached a particularly shrieky section of his sonata, and the children had to lean forward to one another in order to continue their conversation. 'If we go and see Nero first thing tomorrow morning,' Violet said, 'we can talk to him alone, without Olaf butting in. We'll ask him to use the computer. Nero might not believe us, but the computer should be able to convince him to at least investigate Coach Genghis.'

'Maybe Nero will make him take off the turban,' Isadora said, 'revealing Olaf's only eyebrow.'

'Or take off those expensive-looking running shoes,' Klaus said, 'revealing Olaf's tattoo.'

'But if you talk to Nero,' Duncan said, 'then Coach Genghis will know that you're suspicious.'

'That's why we'll have to be extra

careful,' Violet said. 'We want Nero to find out about Olaf, without Olaf finding out about us.'

'And in the meantime,' Duncan said, 'Isadora and I will do some investigating ourselves. Perhaps we can spot one of these assistants you've described.'

'That would be very useful,' Violet said, 'if you're sure about wanting to help us.'

'Say no more about it,' Duncan said and patted Violet's hand. And they said no more about it. They didn't say another word about Count Olaf for the rest of Nero's sonata, or while he performed it the second time, or the third time, or the fourth time, or the fifth time, or even the sixth time, by which time it was very, very late at night. The Baudelaire orphans and the Quagmire triplets merely sat in a companionable comfort, a phrase which here means many things, all of them happy even though it is quite difficult to be happy while hearing a terrible sonata performed over and over by a man who cannot play the violin, while attending an atrocious boarding school with an evil man sitting nearby undoubtedly planning something dreadful. But happy moments came rarely and unexpectedly in the Baudelaires' lives, and the three siblings had learned to accept them. Duncan kept his hand on Violet's and talked to her about terrible concerts he had attended back when the Quagmire parents were alive, and she was happy to hear his stories. Isadora began working on a poem about libraries and showed Klaus what she had written in her notebook, and Klaus was happy to offer suggestions. And Sunny snuggled down in Violet's lap and chewed on the armrest of her seat, happy to bite something that was so sturdy.

I'm sure you would know, even if I didn't tell you, that things were about to get much worse for the Baudelaires, but I will end this chapter with this moment of companionable comfort rather than skip ahead to the unpleasant events of the next morning, or the terrible trials of the days that followed, or the horrific crime that marked the end of the Baudelaires' time at Prufrock Prep. These things happened, of course, and there is no use pretending they didn't. But for now let us ignore the terrible sonata, the dreadul teachers, the nasty, teasing students, and the even more wretched things that will be happening soon enough. Let us enjoy this brief moment of comfort, as the Baudelaires enjoyed it in the company of the Quagmire triplets and, in Sunny's case, an armrest. Let us enjoy, at the end of this chapter, the last happy moment any of these children would have for a long, long time.

CHAPTER SIX

Prufrock Preparatory School is now closed. It has been closed for many years, ever since Mrs. Bass was arrested for bank robbery, and if you were to visit it now, you would find it an empty and silent place. If you walked on the lawn, you would not see any children running around, as there were the day the Baudelaires arrived. If you walked by the building containing the classrooms, you would not hear the droning voice of Mr. Remora telling a story, and if you walked by the building containing the auditorium, you would not hear the scrapings and shriekings of Vice Principal Nero playing the violin. If you went and stood beneath the arch, looking up at the black letters spelling out the name of the school and its austere—a word which here means 'stern and severe'—motto, you would hear nothing but the *swish* of the breeze through the brown and patchy grass.

In short, if you went and visited Prufrock Preparatory School today, the academy would look more or less as it did when the Baudelaires woke up early the next morning and walked to the administrative building to talk to Nero about Coach Genghis. The three children were so anxious to talk to him that they got up especially early, and as they walked across the lawn it felt as if everyone else at Prufrock Prep had slipped away in the middle of the night, leaving the orphans alone amongst the tombstone-shaped buildings. It was an eerie feeling, which is why Violet and Sunny were surprised when Klaus broke the silence by laughing suddenly.

'What are you snickering at?' Violet asked.

'I just realized something,' Klaus said. 'We're going to the administrative building without an appointment. We'll have to eat our meals without silverware.'

'There's nothing funny about that!' Violet said. 'What if they serve oatmeal for breakfast? We'll have to scoop it up with our hands.'

'Oot,' Sunny said, which meant 'Trust me, it's not that difficult,' and at that the Baudelaire sisters joined their brother in laughter. It was not funny, of course, that Nero enforced such terrible punishments, but the idea of eating oatmeal with their hands gave all three siblings the giggles.

'Or fried eggs!' Violet said. 'What if they serve runny fried eggs?'

'Or pancakes, covered in syrup!' Klaus said.

'Soup!' Sunny shrieked, and they all broke out in laughter again.

'Remember the picnic?' Violet said. 'We were going to Rutabaga River for a picnic, and Father was so excited about the meal he made that he forgot to pack silverware!'

'Of course I remember,' Klaus said. 'We had to eat all that sweet-and-sour shrimp with our hands.'

'Sticky!' Sunny said, holding her hands up.

'It sure was,' Violet agreed. 'Afterward, we went to wash our hands in the river, and we found a perfect place to try the fishing rod I made.'

'And I picked blackberries with Mother,' Klaus said.

'Eroos,' Sunny said, which meant something like 'And I bit rocks.'

The children stopped laughing now as they remembered that afternoon, which hadn't been so very long ago but felt like it had happened in the distant, distant past. After the fire, the children had known their parents were dead, of course, but it had felt like they had merely gone away somewhere and would be back before long. Now, remembering the way the sunlight had shone on the water of Rutabaga River and the laughter of their parents as they'd made a mess of themselves eating the sweet-and-sour shrimp, the picnic seemed so far away that they knew their parents were never coming back.

'Maybe we'll go back there,' Violet said quietly. 'Maybe someday we can visit the river again, and catch fish and pick blackberries.'

'Maybe we can,' Klaus said, but the Baudelaires all knew that even if someday they went back to Rutabaga River—which they never did, by the way—that it would not be the same. 'Maybe we can, but in the meantime we've got to talk to Nero. Come on, here's the administrative building.'

The Baudelaires sighed and walked into the building, surrendering the use of Prufrock Prep's silverware. They climbed the stairs to the ninth floor and knocked on Nero's door, surprised that they could not hear him practicing the violin. 'Come in if you must,' Nero said, and the orphans walked in. Nero had his back to the door, looking at his reflection in the window as he tied a rubber band around one of his pigtails. When he was finished, he held both hands up in the air. 'Ladies and gentlemen, Vice Principal Nero!' he announced, and the children began applauding obediently. Nero whirled around.

'I only expected to hear one person clapping,' he said sternly. 'Violet and

Klaus, you're not allowed up here. You know that.'

'I beg your pardon, sir,' Violet said, 'but all three of us have something very important we need to discuss with you.'

'All three of us have something very important we need to discuss with you,' Nero replied in his usual nasty way. 'It must be important for you to sacrifice your silverware privileges. Well, well, out with it. I have a lot of rehearsing to do for my next concert, so don't waste my time.'

'This won't take long,' Klaus promised. He paused before continuing, which is a good thing to do if you're choosing your words very, very carefully. 'We are concerned,' he continued, choosing his words very, very carefully, 'that Count Olaf may have somehow managed to get to Prufrock Prep.'

'Nonsense,' Nero said. 'Now go away and let me practice the violin.'

'But it might not be nonsense,' Violet said. 'Olaf is a master of disguise. He could be right under our very noses and we wouldn't know it.'

85

'The only thing under *my* nose,' Nero said, 'is my mouth, which is telling you to leave.'

'Count Olaf could be Mr. Remora,' Klaus said. 'Or Mrs. Bass.'

'Mr. Remora and Mrs. Bass have taught at this school for more than forty -seven years,' Nero said dismissively. 'I would know if one of them were in disguise.'

'What about the people who work at the cafeteria?' Violet asked. 'They're always wearing those metal masks.'

'Those are for safety, not for disguises,' Nero said. 'You brats have some very silly ideas. Next you'll be saying that Count Olaf has disguised himself as your boyfriend, what's-his-name, the triplet.'

Violet blushed. 'Duncan Quagmire is not my boyfriend,' she said, 'and he's not Count Olaf, either.'

But Nero was too busy making idiotic jokes to listen. 'Who knows?' he asked, and then laughed again. 'Hee hee hee. Maybe he's disguised himself as Carmelita Spats.'

'Or me!' came a voice from the

doorway. The Baudelaires whirled around and saw Coach Genghis standing there with a red rose in his hand and a fierce look in his eye.

'Or you!' Nero said. 'Hee hee hee. Imagine this Olaf fellow pretending to be the finest gym teacher in the country.'

Klaus looked at Coach Genghis and thought of all the trouble he had caused, whether he was pretending to be Uncle Monty's assistant Stefano, or Captain Sham, or Shirley, or any of the other phony names he had used. Klaus wanted desperately to say 'You *are* Count Olaf!' but he knew that if the Baudelaires pretended that Coach Genghis was fooling them, they had a better chance of revealing his plan, whatever it was. So he bit his tongue, a phrase which here means that he simply kept quiet. He did not actually bite his tongue, but opened his mouth and laughed. 'That would be funny!' he lied. 'Imagine if you were really Count Olaf! Wouldn't that be funny, Coach Genghis? That would mean that your turban would really be a disguise!'

'My turban?' Coach Genghis said. His fierce look melted away as he realized—incorrectly, of course—that Klaus was joking. 'A disguise? Ho ho ho!'

'Hee hee hee!' Nero laughed.

Violet and Sunny both saw at once what Klaus was doing, and they followed suit. 'Oh yes, Genghis,' Violet cried, as if she were joking, 'take your turban off and show us the one eyebrow you are hiding! Ha ha ha!'

'You three children are really quite funny!' Nero cried. 'You're like three professional comedians!'

'Volasocks!' Sunny shrieked, showing all four teeth in a fake smile.

'Oh yes,' Klaus said. 'Sunny is right! If you were really Olaf in disguise, then your running shoes would be covering your tattoo!'

'Hee hee hee!' Nero said. 'You children are like three clowns!'

'Ho ho ho!' Count Olaf said.

'Ha ha ha!' Violet said, who was beginning to feel queasy from faking all this laughter. Looking up at Genghis, and smiling so hard that her teeth

88

ached, she stood on tiptoe and tried to reach his turban. 'I'm going to rip this off,' she said, as if she were still joking, 'and show off your one eyebrow!'

'Hee hee hee!' Nero said, shaking his pigtails in laughter. 'You're like three trained monkeys!'

Klaus crouched down to the ground and grabbed one of Genghis's feet. 'And I'm going to rip your shoes off,' he said, as if *he* were still joking, 'and show off your tattoo!'

'Hee hee hee!' Nero said. 'You're like three—'

The Baudelaires didn't get to hear what they were three of, because Coach Genghis stuck out both of his arms, catching Klaus with one hand and Violet with the other. 'Ho ho ho!' he said, and then abruptly stopped laughing. 'Of course,' he said in a tone of voice that was suddenly serious, 'I can't take off my running shoes, because I've been exercising and my feet smell, and I can't take off my turban for religious reasons.

'Hee hee—' Nero stopped giggling and became very serious himself. 'Oh,

Coach Genghis,' he said, 'we wouldn't ask you to violate your religious beliefs, and I certainly don't want your feet stinking up my office.'

Violet struggled to reach the turban and Klaus struggled to remove one of the evil coach's shoes, but Genghis held them both tight.

'Drat!' Sunny shrieked.

'Joke time is over!' Nero announced. 'Thank you for brightening up my morning, children. Good-bye, and enjoy your breakfast without silverware! Now, Coach Genghis, what can I do for you?'

'Well, Nero,' Genghis said, 'I just wanted to give you this rose—a small gift of congratulations for the wonderful concert you gave us last night!'

'Oh, thank you,' Nero said, taking the rose out of Genghis's hand and giving it a good smell. 'I *was* wonderful, wasn't I?'

'You were *perfection*!' Genghis said. 'The first time you played your sonata, I was deeply moved. The second time, I had tears in my eyes. The third time, I was sobbing. The fourth time, I had an uncontrollable emotional attack. The fifth time—'

The Baudelaires did not hear about the fifth time because Nero's door swung shut behind them. They looked at one another in dismay. The Baudelaires had come very close to revealing Coach Genghis's disguise, but close was not enough. They trudged silently out of the administrative building and over to the cafeteria. Evidently, Nero had already called the metal-masked cafeteria workers, because when Violet and Klaus reached the end of the line, the workers refused to hand them any silverware. Prufrock Prep was not serving oatmeal for breakfast, but Violet and Klaus knew that eating scrambled eggs with their hands was not going to be very pleasant.

'Oh, don't worry about that,' Isadora said when the children slid glumly into seats beside the Quagmires. 'Here, Klaus and I will take turns with my silverware, and you can share with Duncan, Violet. Tell us how everything went in Nero's office.'

'Not very well,' Violet admitted.

'Coach Genghis got there right after we did, and we didn't want him to see that we knew who he really was.'

Isadora pulled her notebook out of her pocket and read out loud to her friends.

'It would be a stroke of luck
if Coach Genghis were hit by a truck,'

she read. 'That's my latest poem. I know it's not that helpful, but I thought you might like to hear it anyway.'

'I did like hearing it,' Klaus said. 'And it certainly *would* be a stroke of luck if that happened. But I wouldn't bet on it.'

'Well, we'll think of another plan,' Duncan said, handing Violet his fork.

'I hope so,' Violet said. 'Count Olaf doesn't usually wait very long to put his evil schemes into action.'

'Kosbal!' Sunny shrieked.

'Does Sunny mean "I have a plan"?' Isadora asked. 'I'm trying to get the hang of her way of talking.'

'I think she means something more like "Here comes Carmelita Spats,"'

Klaus said, pointing across the cafeteria. Sure enough, Carmelita Spats was walking toward their table with a big, smug smile on her face.

'Hello, you cakesniffers,' she said. 'I have a message for you from Coach Genghis. I get to be his Special Messenger because I'm the cutest, prettiest, nicest girl in the whole school.'

'Oh, stop bragging, Carmelita,' Duncan said.

'You're just jealous,' Carmelita replied, 'because Coach Genghis likes me best instead of you.'

'I couldn't care less about Coach Genghis,' Duncan said. 'Just deliver your message and leave us alone.'

'The message is this,' Carmelita said. 'The three Baudelaire orphans are to report to the front lawn tonight, immediately after dinner.'

'After dinner?' Violet said. 'But after dinner we're supposed to go to Nero's violin recital.'

'That's the message,' Carmelita insisted. 'He said that if you don't show up you'll be in big trouble, so if I were you, Violet—'

'You *aren't* Violet, thank goodness,' Duncan interrupted. It is not very polite to interrupt a person, of course, but sometimes if the person is very unpleasant you can hardly stop yourself. 'Thank you for your message. Good-bye.'

'It is traditional,' Carmelita said, 'to give a Special Messenger a tip after she has delivered a message.'

'If you don't leave us alone,' Isadora said, 'you're going to get a headful of scrambled eggs as a tip.'

'You're just a jealous cakesniffer,' Carmelita sneered, but she left the Baudelaires and Quagmires alone.

'Don't worry,' Duncan said when he was sure Carmelita couldn't hear him. 'It's still morning. We have all day to figure out what to do. Here, have another spoonful of eggs, Violet.'

'No, thank you,' Violet said. 'I don't have much of an appetite.' And it was true. None of the Baudelaires had an appetite. Scrambled eggs had never been the siblings' favorite dish, particularly Sunny, who much preferred food she could really sink her teeth into, but their lack of appetite had nothing to do with the eggs. It had to do with Coach Genghis, of course, and the message that he had sent to them. It had to do with the thought of meeting him on the lawn, after dinner, all alone. Duncan was right that it was still morning, and that they had all day to figure out what to do. But it did not feel like morning. Violet, Klaus, and Sunny sat in the cafeteria, not taking another bite of their breakfast, and it felt like the sun had already set. It felt like night had already fallen, and that Coach Genghis was already waiting for them. It was only morning, and the Baudelaire orphans already felt like they were in his clutches.

CHAPTER SEVEN

The Baudelaire orphans' schoolday was particularly austere, a word which here means that Mr. Remora's stories were particularly boring, Mrs. Bass's obsession with the metric system was particularly irritating, and Nero's administrative demands were particularly difficult, but Violet, Klaus, and Sunny did not really notice. Violet sat at her schooldesk, and anybody who did not know Violet would have thought that she was paying close attention, because her hair was tied up in a ribbon to keep it out of her eyes. But Violet's thoughts were far, far away from the dull tales Mr. Remora was telling. She had tied her hair up, of course, to help focus her keen inventing brain on the problem that was facing the Baudelaires, and she didn't want to waste an ounce of her attention on the rambling, banana-eating man in the front of the room.

Mrs. Bass had brought in a box of pencils for her class and was having them figure out if one of them was any longer or shorter than the rest. And if Mrs. Bass weren't so busy pacing around the room shouting 'Measure!' she might have looked at Klaus and thought that perhaps he shared her obsession with measurement, because his eyes were sharply focused as if he were concentrating. But Klaus was spending the morning on autopilot, a word which here means 'measuring pencils without really thinking about them.' As he placed pencil after pencil next to his ruler, he was thinking of books he had read that might be helpful for their situation.

And if Vice Principal Nero had stopped practicing his violin and looked in on his infant secretary, he would have guessed that Sunny was working very hard, mailing letters he had dictated to various candy companies complaining about their candy quality. But even though Sunny was typing, stapling, and stamping as quickly as she could, her mind was not on secretarial supplies but on the appointment she and her siblings had with Coach Genghis that evening, and what they could do about it.

The Quagmires were curiously absent from lunch, so the Baudelaires were really forced to eat with their hands this time, but as they picked up handfuls of spaghetti and tried to eat them as neatly as possible the three children were thinking so hard that they barely spoke. They knew, almost without discussing the matter, that none of them had been able to guess Coach Genghis's plan, and that they hadn't figured out a way to avoid their appointment with him on the lawn, an appointment that drew closer and closer with every handful of lunch. The Baudelaires passed the afternoon in more or less the same way, ignoring Mr. Remora's stories, Mrs. Bass's pencils, and the diminishing supply of staples, and even during gym period—one of Carmelita's bratty friends informed them that Genghis would start teaching the next day, but in the meantime they were to run around as usual—the three children raced around the lawn in utter silence, devoting all of their brainpower to thinking about their situation.

The Baudelaires had been so very quiet, and thinking so very hard, that when the Quagmires sat down across from them at dinnertime and said in unison, 'We've solved your problem,' it was more of a startle than a relief.

'Goodness,' Violet said. 'You startled me.'

'I thought you'd be relieved,' Duncan said. 'Didn't you hear us? We said we've solved your problem.'

'We're startled *and* relieved,' Klaus said. 'What do you mean, you've solved our problem? My sisters and I have been thinking about it all day, and we've gotten nowhere. We don't know what Coach Genghis is up to, although we're sure he's up to something. And we don't know how we can avoid meeting him after dinner, although we're sure that he'll do something terrible if we do.'

'At first I thought he might simply be planning to kidnap us,' Violet said, 'but he wouldn't have to be in disguise to do that.'

'And at first I thought we should call Mr. Poe after all,' Klaus said, 'and tell him what's going on. But if Count Olaf can fool an advanced computer, he'll surely be able to fool an average banker.'

'Tobricia!' Sunny said in agreement.

'Duncan and I have been thinking about it all day, too,' Isadora said. 'I filled up five and a half pages of my notebook writing down possible ideas, and Duncan filled up three.'

'I write smaller,' Duncan explained, handing his fork to Violet so she could take her turn at the meat loaf they were having for dinner.

'Right before lunch, we compared notes,' Isadora continued, 'and the two

100

of us had the same idea. So we sneaked away and put our plan into action.'

'That's why we weren't at lunch,' Duncan explained. 'You'll notice that there are puddles of beverages on our tray instead of glasses.'

'Well, you can share *our* glasses,' Klaus said, handing his to Isadora, 'just like you're letting us share your silverware. But what is your plan? What did you put into action?'

Duncan and Isadora looked at one another, smiled, and leaned in close to the Baudelaires so they could be sure no one would overhear.

'We propped open the back door of the auditorium,' Duncan said. He and Isadora smiled triumphantly and leaned back in their chairs. The Baudelaires did not feel triumphant. They felt confused. They did not want to insult their friends, who had broken the rules and sacrificed their drinking glasses just to help them, but they were unable to see how propping open the back door of the auditorium was a solution to the trouble in which they found themselves.

'I'm sorry,' Violet said after a pause. 'I don't understand how propping open the back door of the auditorium solves our problem.'

'Don't you see?' Isadora asked. 'We're going to sit in the back of the auditorium tonight, and as soon as Nero begins his concert, we will tiptoe out and sneak over to the front lawn. That way we can keep an eye on you and Coach Genghis. If anything fishy happens, we will run back to the concert and alert Vice Principal Nero.'

'It's the perfect plan, don't you think?' Duncan asked. 'I'm rather proud of my sister and me, if I do say so myself.'

The Baudelaire children looked at one another doubtfully. They didn't want to disappoint their friends or criticize the plan that the Quagmire triplets had cooked up, particularly since the Baudelaires hadn't cooked up any plan themselves. But Count Olaf was so evil and so clever that the three siblings couldn't help but think that propping a door open and sneaking out to spy on him was not much of a defense against his treachery.

'We appreciate you trying to solve our problem,' Klaus said gently, 'but Count Olaf is an extremely treacherous person. He always has something up his sleeve. I wouldn't want you to get into any danger on our behalf.'

'Don't talk nonsense,' Isadora said firmly, taking a sip from Violet's glass. 'You're the ones in danger, and it's up to us to help you. And we're not frightened of Olaf. I'm confident this plan is a good one.'

The Baudelaires looked at one another again. It was very brave of the Quagmire triplets not to be frightened of Olaf and to be so confident about their plan. But the three siblings could not help but wonder if the Quagmires should be so brave. Olaf was such a wretched man that it seemed wise to be frightened of him, and he had defeated so many of the Baudelaires' plans that it seemed a little foolish to be so confident about this one. But the children were so appreciative of their friends' efforts that they said nothing more about the matter. In the years to come, the Baudelaire orphans would regret this, this time when they said nothing more about the matter, but in the meantime they merely finished their dinner with the Quagmires, passing silverware and drinking glasses back and forth and trying to talk about other things. They discussed other projects they might do to improve the Orphans Shack, and what other matters they might research in the library, and what they could do about Sunny's problem with the staples, which were running out quite rapidly, and before they knew it dinner was over. The Quagmires hurried off to the violin recital, promising to sneak out as quickly as they could, and the Baudelaires walked out of the cafeteria and over to the front lawn.

The last few rays of the sunset made the children cast long, long shadows as they walked, as if the Baudelaires had been stretched across the brown grass by some horrible mechanical device. The children looked down at their shadows, which looked as flimsy as sheets of paper, and wished with every

104

step that they could do something else—*anything* else—other than meet Coach Genghis alone on the front lawn. They wished they could just keep walking, under the arch, past the front lawn, and out into the world, but where could they go? The three orphans were all alone in the world. Their parents were dead. Their banker was too busy to take good care of them. And their only friends were two more orphans, who the Baudelaires sincerely hoped had snuck out of the recital by now and were spying on them as they approached the solitary figure of Coach Genghis, waiting for them impatiently on the edge of the lawn. The waning light of the sunset—the word 'waning' here means 'dim, and making everything look extra-creepy'— made the shadow of the coach's turban look like a huge, deep hole.

'You're late,' Genghis said in his scratchy voice. As the siblings reached him, they could see that he had both hands behind his back as if he were hiding something. 'Your instructions were to be here right after dinner, and you're late.'

'We're very sorry,' Violet said, craning her neck to try and catch a glimpse of what was behind his back. 'It took us a little longer to eat our dinner without silverware.'

'If you were smart,' Genghis said, 'you would have borrowed the silverware of one of your friends.'

'We never thought of that,' Klaus said. When one is forced to tell atrocious lies, one often feels a guilty flutter in one's stomach, and Klaus felt such a flutter now. 'You certainly are an intelligent man,' he continued.

'Not only am I intelligent,' Genghis agreed, 'but I'm also very smart. Now, let's get right to work. Even stupid children like yourselves should remember what I said about orphans having excellent bone structure for running. That's why you are about to do Special Orphan Running Exercises, or S.O.R.E. for short.'

'Ooladu!' Sunny shrieked.

'My sister means that sounds exciting,' Violet said, although 'Ooladu!' actually meant 'I wish you'd tell us what you're *really* up to, Genghis.'

'I'm glad you're so enthusiastic,' Genghis said. 'In certain cases, enthusiasm can make up for a lack of brainpower.' He took his hands from behind his back, and the children saw that he was holding a large metal can and a long, prickly brush. The can was open, and an eerie white glow was shining out of the top. 'Now, before we begin S.O.R.E., we'll need a track. This is luminous paint, which means it glows in the dark.'

'How interesting,' Klaus said, although he'd known what the word 'luminous' means for two and a half years.

'Well, if you find it so interesting,' Genghis said, his eyes looking as luminous as the paint, 'you can be in charge of the brush. *Here.*' He thrust the long, prickly brush into Klaus's hands. 'And you little girls can hold the paint can. I want you to paint a big circle on the grass so you can see where you are running when you start your laps. Go on, what are you waiting for?'

The Baudelaires looked at one

another. What they were waiting for, of course, was Genghis revealing what he was really up to with the paint, the brush, and the ridiculous Special Orphan Running Exercises. But in the meantime, they figured they'd better do as Genghis said. Painting a big, luminous circle on the lawn didn't seem to be particularly dangerous, so Violet picked up the paint can, and Klaus dipped the brush into the paint and began making a big circle. For the moment, Sunny was something of a fifth wheel, a phrase which means 'not in a position to do anything particularly helpful,' but she crawled alongside her siblings, offering moral support.

'Bigger!' Genghis called out in the dark. 'Wider!' The Baudelaires followed his instructions and made the circle bigger and wider, walking farther away from Genghis and leaving a glowing trail of paint. They looked out into the gloom of the evening, wondering where the Quagmire triplets were hiding, or if indeed they had managed to sneak out of the recital at all. But the sun was down now, and the

only thing the orphans could see was the bright circle of light they were painting on the lawn and the dim figure of Genghis, his white turban looking like a floating skull in the night. 'Bigger! Wider! All right, all right, that's big and wide enough! Finish the circle where I am standing! Hurry up!'

'What do you think we're *really* doing?' Violet whispered to her brother.

'I don't know,' Klaus said. 'I've only read three or four books on paint. I know that paint can sometimes be poisonous or cause birth defects. But Genghis isn't making us eat the circle, and you're not pregnant, of course, so I can't imagine.'

Sunny wanted to add 'Gargaba!' which meant 'Maybe the luminous paint is serving as some sort of glowing signal,' but the Baudelaires had come full circle and were too close to Genghis to do any more talking.

'I suppose that will do, orphans,' Genghis said, snatching the brush and the can of paint out of their hands. 'Now, take your marks, and when I blow my whistle, begin running around the circle you've made until I tell you to stop.'

'What?' Violet said. As I'm sure you know, there are two types of 'What?' in the world. The first type simply means 'Excuse me, I didn't hear you. Could you please repeat yourself?' The second type is a little trickier. It means something more along the lines of 'Excuse me, I did hear you, but I can't believe that's really what you meant,' and this second type is obviously the type Violet was using at this moment. She was standing right next to Genghis, so she'd obviously heard what had come out of the smelly mouth of this miserable man. But she couldn't believe that Genghis was simply going to make them run laps. He was such a sneaky and revolting person that the eldest Baudelaire simply could not accept that his scheme was only as evil as the average gym class.

'*What?*' Genghis repeated in a mocking way. He had obviously taken a page out of Nero's book, a phrase which here means 'learned how to repeat things in a mocking way, in order to make fun of children.' 'I know you heard me, little orphan girl. You're standing right next to me. Now take your marks, all of you, and begin running as soon as I blow my whistle.'

'But Sunny is a baby,' Klaus protested. 'She can't really run, at least not professionally.'

'Then she may crawl as fast as she can,' Genghis replied. 'Now—on your marks, get set, *go!*'

Genghis blew his whistle and the Baudelaire orphans began to run, pacing themselves so they could run together even though they had different-sized legs. They finished one lap, and then another, and then another and another and then five more and then another and then seven more and then another and then three more and then two more and then another and then another and then six more and then they lost track. Coach Genghis kept blowing his whistle and occasionally shouted tedious and unhelpful things like 'Keep running!' or 'Another lap!' The children looked down at the luminous circle so they could stay in a circle, and the children looked over at Genghis as he grew fainter and then clearer as they finished a lap, and the children looked out into the darkness to see if they could catch a glimpse of the Quagmires.

The Baudelaires also looked at one another from time to time, but they didn't speak, not even when they were far enough away from Genghis that he could not overhear. One reason they did not speak was to conserve energy, because although the Baudelaires were in reasonably good shape, they had not run so many laps in their lives, and before too long they were breathing too hard to really discuss anything. But the other reason they did not speak was that Violet had already spoken for them when she had asked the second type of 'What?' Coach Genghis kept blowing his whistle, and the children kept running around and around the track, and echoing in each of their minds was this second, trickier type of question. The three siblings had heard

Coach Genghis, but they couldn't believe that S.O.R.E. was the extent of his evil plan. The Baudelaire orphans kept running around the glowing circle until the first rays of sunrise began to reflect on the jewel in Genghis's turban, and all they could think was *What? What? What?*

CHAPTER EIGHT

'What?' Isadora asked.

'I said, "Finally, as the sun rose, Coach Genghis had us stop running laps and let us go to bed,"' Klaus said.

'My sister didn't mean that she didn't hear you,' Duncan explained. 'She meant that she heard you, but she didn't believe that's really what you meant. And to tell you the truth, I can scarcely believe it myself, even though I saw it with my own eyes.'

'I can't believe it either,' Violet said, wincing as she took a bite of the salad that the masked people had served for lunch. It was the next afternoon, and all three Baudelaire orphans were doing a great deal of wincing, a word which here means 'frowning in pain, alarm, or distress.' When Coach Genghis had called last night's activities S.O.R.E., he had merely used the name as an acronym for Special Orphan Running Exercises, but the three children thought that the name S.O.R.E. was even more appropriate than that. After a full night of S.O.R.E., they'd been sore all day. Their legs were sore from all their running. When they'd finally entered the Orphans Shack to go to sleep, they had been too tired to put on their noisy shoes, so their toes were sore from the claws of the tiny territorial crabs. And their heads were sore, not only from headaches, which often occur when one doesn't get enough sleep, but also from trying to figure out what Coach Genghis was up to in making them run all those laps. The Baudelaire legs were sore, the Baudelaire toes were sore, the Baudelaire heads were sore, and soon the muscles on the sides of the Baudelaire mouths would be sore from wincing all day long.

It was lunchtime, and the three

children were trying to discuss the previous evening with the Quagmire triplets, who weren't very sore and not nearly as tired. One reason was that they had been hiding behind the archway, spying on Genghis and the Baudelaires, instead of running around and around the luminous circle. The other reason was that the Quagmires had done their spying in shifts. After the Baudelaires had run the first few laps and there was no sign of them stopping, the two triplets had decided to alternate between Duncan sleeping and Isadora spying, and Duncan spying and Isadora sleeping. The two siblings promised each other that they would wake up the sleeping one if the spying one noticed anything unusual.

'I had the last shift,' Duncan explained, 'so my sister didn't see the end of S.O.R.E. But it doesn't matter. All that happened was that Coach Genghis had you stop running laps and let you go to bed. I thought that he might insist on getting your fortune before you could stop running.'

'And I thought that the luminous

circle would serve as a landing strip,' Isadora said, 'for a helicopter, piloted by one of his assistants, to swoop down and take you away. The only thing I couldn't figure out was why you had to run all those laps before the helicopter showed up.'

'But the helicopter didn't show up,' Klaus said, taking a sip of water and wincing. 'Nothing showed up.'

'Maybe the pilot got lost,' Isadora said.

'Or maybe Coach Genghis became as tired as you did, and forgot to ask for your fortune,' Duncan said.

Violet shook her sore head. 'He would never get too tired to get our fortune,' she said. 'He's up to something, that much is for sure, but I just can't figure out what it is.'

'Of course you can't figure it out,' Duncan said. 'You're exhausted. I'm glad Isadora and I thought of spying in shifts. We're going to use all our spare time to investigate. We'll go through all of our notes, and do some more research in the library. There must be something that can help us figure

118

it out.'

'I'll do research, too,' Klaus said, yawning. 'I'm quite good at it.'

'I know you are,' Isadora said, smiling. 'But not today, Klaus. We'll work on uncovering Genghis's plan, and you three can catch up on your sleep. You're too tired to do much good in a library or anywhere else.'

Violet and Klaus looked at each other's tired faces, and then down at their baby sister, and they saw that the Quagmire triplets were right. Violet had been so tired that she had taken only a few notes on Mr. Remora's painfully dull stories. Klaus had been so tired that he had incorrectly measured nearly all of Mrs. Bass's objects. And although Sunny had not reported what she had done that morning in Nero's office, she couldn't have been a very good administrative assistant, because she had fallen asleep right there in the cafeteria, her little head on her salad, as if it were a soft pillow instead of leaves of lettuce, slices of tomato, gobs of creamy honey-mustard dressing, and crispy croutons, which are small toasted pieces of bread that give a salad some added crunch. Violet gently lifted her sister's head out of the salad and shook a few croutons out of her hair. Sunny winced, made a faint, miserable noise, and went back to sleep in Violet's lap. 'Perhaps you're right, Isadora,' Violet said. 'We'll stumble through the afternoon somehow and get a good night's sleep tonight. If we're lucky, Vice Principal Nero will play something quiet at tonight's concert and we can sleep through that as well.'

You can see, with that last sentence, just how tired Violet really was, because 'if we're lucky' is not a phrase that she, or either of her siblings, used very often. The reason, of course, is quite clear: the Baudelaire orphans were not lucky. Smart, yes. Charming, yes. Able to survive austere situations, yes. But the children were not lucky, and so wouldn't use the phrase 'if we're lucky' any more than they would use the phrase 'if we're stalks of celery,' because neither phrase was appropriate. If the Baudelaire orphans had been stalks of celery, they would not have been small children in great distress, and if they had been lucky, Carmelita Spats would not have approached their table at this particular moment and delivered another unfortunate message.

'Hello, you cakesniffers,' she said, 'although judging from the baby brat you're more like saladsniffers. I have another message for you from Coach Genghis. I get to be his Special Messenger because I'm the cutest, prettiest, nicest little girl in the whole school.'

'If you were really the nicest person in the whole school,' Isadora said, 'you wouldn't make fun of a sleeping infant. But never mind, what is the message?'

'It's actually the same one as last time,' Carmelita said, 'but I'll repeat it in case you're too stupid to remember. The three Baudelaire orphans are to report to the front lawn tonight, immediately after dinner.'

'What?' Klaus asked.

'Are you *deaf* as well as cakesniffy?' Carmelita asked. 'I said—'

'Yes, yes, Klaus heard you,' Isadora said quickly. 'He didn't mean that kind of "What?" We have received the message, Carmelita. Now please go away.'

'That's two tips you owe me,' Carmelita said, but she flounced off.

'I can't believe it,' Violet said. 'Not more laps! My legs are almost too sore to walk, let alone run.'

'Carmelita didn't say anything about more laps,' Duncan pointed out. 'Maybe Coach Genghis is putting his real plan into action tonight. In any case, we'll sneak out of the recital again and keep an eye on you.'

'In shifts,' Isadora added, nodding in agreement. 'And I bet we'll have a clear picture of his plan by then. We have the rest of the day to do research.' Isadora paused, and flipped open her black notebook to the right page. She read,

'Don't worry Baudelaires, don't
feel disgrace—
The Quagmire triplets are on the case.'

'Thank you,' Klaus said, giving

Isadora a tired smile of appreciation. 'My sisters and I are thankful for all your help. And we're going to put our minds to the problem, even though we're too exhausted to do research. If we're lucky, all of us working together can defeat Coach Genghis.'

There was that phrase again, 'if we're lucky,' coming out of the mouth of a Baudelaire, and once again it felt about as appropriate as 'if we're stalks of celery.' The only difference was that the Baudelaire orphans did not wish to be stalks of celery. While it is true that if they were stalks of celery they would not be orphans because celery is a plant and so cannot really be said to have parents, Violet, Klaus, and Sunny did not wish to be the stringy, low-calorie vegetable. Unfortunate things can happen to celery as easily as they can happen to children. Celery can be sliced into small pieces and dipped into clam dip at fancy parties. It can be coated in peanut butter and served as a snack. It can merely sit in a field and rot away, if the nearby celery farmers are lazy or on vacation. All these terrible things can happen to celery, and the orphans knew it, so if you were to ask the Baudelaires if they wanted to be stalks of celery they would say of course not. But they wanted to be lucky. The Baudelaires did not necessarily want to be extremely lucky, like someone who finds a treasure map or someone who wins a lifetime supply of ice cream in a contest, or like the man—and not, alas, me—who was lucky enough to marry my beloved Beatrice, and live with her in happiness over the course of her short life. But the Baudelaires wanted to be lucky enough. They wanted to be lucky enough to figure out how to escape Coach Genghis's clutches, and it seemed that being lucky would be their only chance. Violet was too tired to invent anything, and Klaus was too tired to read anything, and Sunny, still asleep in Violet's lap, was too tired to bite anything or anybody, and it seemed that even with the diligence of the Quagmire triplets—the word 'diligence' here means 'ability to take good notes in dark green and pitch-black notebooks'—they needed to be lucky if they wanted to stay alive. The Baudelaires huddled together as if the cafeteria were extremely cold, wincing in soreness and worry. It seemed to the Baudelaire orphans that they wanted to be lucky more than they had in their entire lives.

CHAPTER NINE

Occasionally, events in one's life become clearer through the prism of experience, a phrase which simply means that things tend to become clearer as time goes on. For instance, when a person is just born, they usually have no idea what curtains are and spend a great deal of their first months wondering why on earth Mommy and Daddy have hung large pieces of cloth over each window in the nursery. But as the person grows older, the idea of curtains becomes clearer through the prism of experience. The person will learn the word 'curtains' and notice that they are actually quite handy for keeping a room dark when it is time to sleep, and for decorating an otherwise boring window area. Eventually, they will entirely accept the idea of curtains, and may even purchase some curtains of their own, or venetian blinds, and it is all due to the prism of experience.

Coach Genghis's S.O.R.E. program, however, was one event that didn't seem to get any clearer at all through the Baudelaire orphans' prism of experience. If anything, it grew even harder and harder to understand, because Violet, Klaus, and Sunny became so utterly exhausted as the days—and, more particularly, the nights—wore on. After the children received their second message from Carmelita Spats, they spent the rest of the afternoon wondering what Coach Genghis would make them do that evening. The Quagmire triplets wondered along with them, so everyone was surprised—the Baudelaires, who met Genghis out on the front lawn after dinner again, and the Quagmires, who tiptoed out of the recital and spied on them, in shifts, from behind the archway again—when Genghis began blowing his whistle and ordered the Baudelaire orphans to begin running. The Baudelaires and Quagmires thought that surely Genghis would do something far more sinister than more laps.

But while a second evening of running laps might have lacked in sinisterity, Violet, Klaus, and Sunny were too exhausted to notice. They could scarcely hear the shrieks of Genghis's whistle and his cries of 'Keep running!' and 'Another lap!' over the sound of their own desperate panting for breath. They grew so sweaty that the orphans thought they would give up the entire Baudelaire fortune for a good long shower. And their legs grew so sore that the children forgot, even with their prism of experience, what it felt like to have legs that didn't ache from thigh to toe.

Lap after lap the Baudelaires ran, hardly taking their eyes off the circle of luminous paint that still glowed brightly on the darkening lawn, and staring at this circle was somehow the worst part of all. As the evening turned to night, the luminous circle was all the Baudelaires could really see, and it imprinted itself into their eyes so they could see it even when they were staring desperately into the darkness. If you've ever had a flash photograph taken, and the blob of the flash has stayed in your view for a few moments afterward, then you are familiar with what was happening to the Baudelaires, except the glowing circle stayed in their minds for so long that it became symbolic. The word 'symbolic' here means that the glowing circle felt like it stood for more than merely a track, and what it stood for was zero. The luminous zero glowed in the Baudelaire minds, and it was symbolic of what they knew of their situation. They knew zero about what Genghis was up to. They knew zero about why they were running endless laps. And they had zero energy to think about it.

Finally, the sun began to rise, and Coach Genghis dismissed his orphan track team. The Baudelaires stumbled blearily to the Orphans Shack, too tired to even see if Duncan and Isadora were sneaking back to their dormitory after their last shift of spying. Once again, the three siblings were too tired to put on their noisy shoes, so their toes were doubly sore when they awoke, just two hours later, to begin another groggy day. But—and I shudder to tell you this—this was not the last groggy day for the Baudelaire orphans. The dreadful Carmelita Spats delivered them the usual message at lunch, after they spent the morning dozing through classes and secretarial duties, and the Baudelaires put their heads on the cafeteria table in despair at the idea of another night of running. The Quagmires tried to comfort them, promising to double their research efforts, but Violet, Klaus, and Sunny were too tired for conversation, even with their closest friends. Luckily, their closest friends understood completely and didn't find the Baudelaires' silence rude or discouraging.

It seems impossible to believe that the three Baudelaires managed to survive another evening of S.O.R.E., but in times of extreme stress one can often find energy hidden in even the most exhausted areas of the body. I discovered this myself when I was woken up in the middle of the night and chased sixteen miles by an angry mob armed with torches, swords, and vicious dogs, and the Baudelaire orphans discovered it as they ran laps, not only for that night but also for six nights following. This made a grand total of nine S.O.R.E. sessions, although 'grand' would seem to be the wrong word for endless evenings of desperate panting, sweaty bodies, and achy legs. For nine nights, the Baudelaire brains were plagued with the symbolic, luminous zero glowing in their minds like a giant donut of despair.

As the Baudelaire orphans suffered, their schoolwork suffered with them. As I'm sure you know, a good night's sleep helps you perform well in school, and so if you are a student you should always get a good night's sleep unless you have come to the good part of your book, and then you should stay up all night and let your schoolwork fall by the wayside, a phrase which means 'flunk.' In the days that followed, the Baudelaires were much more exhausted than somebody who had stayed up all night reading, and their schoolwork did more than fall by the wayside. It fell *off* the wayside, a phrase which here has different meanings for each child. For Violet, it meant that she was so drowsy that she did not write down a single word of Mr. Remora's stories. For Klaus, it meant that he was so weary that he didn't measure a single one of Mrs. Bass's objects. And for Sunny, it meant that she was so exhausted that she didn't do anything Vice Principal Nero assigned her to do. The Baudelaire orphans believed that doing well in school was extremely important, even if the school happened to be run by a tyrannical idiot, but they were simply too fatigued from their nightly laps to do their assigned work. Before long, the circle of luminous paint was not the only zero the Baudelaires saw. Violet saw a zero at the top of her paper when she was unable to recall any of Mr. Remora's stories for a test. Klaus saw a zero in Mrs. Bass's gradebook when he was called on to report the exact length of a tube sock he was supposed to be measuring and was discovered to be taking a nap instead. And Sunny saw a zero when she checked the staple drawer and saw that there were zero staples inside.

'This is getting ridiculous,' Isadora said when Sunny updated her siblings and friends at the start of another weary lunch. 'Look at you, Sunny. It was inappropriate to hire you as an administrative assistant in the first place, and it's simply absurd to have you crawl laps by night and make your own staples by day.'

'Don't call my sister absurd or ridiculous!' Klaus cried.

'I'm not calling *her* ridiculous!' Isadora said. 'I'm calling the *situation* ridiculous!'

'Ridiculous means you want to laugh at it,' said Klaus, who was never too tired to define words, 'and I don't want you laughing at us.'

'I'm not laughing at you,' Isadora

133

said. 'I'm trying to help.'

Klaus snatched his drinking glass from Isadora's side of the table. 'Well, laughing at us doesn't help at all, you cakesniffer.'

Isadora snatched her silverware from Klaus's hands. 'Calling me names doesn't help either, Klaus.'

'Mumdum!' Sunny shrieked.

'Oh, stop it, both of you,' Duncan said. 'Isadora, can't you see that Klaus is just tired? And Klaus, can't you see that Isadora is just frustrated?'

Klaus took his glasses off and returned his drinking glass to Isadora. 'I'm too tired to see anything,' he said. 'I'm sorry, Isadora. Being tired makes me crabby. In a few days I'll turn as nasty as Carmelita Spats.'

Isadora handed her silverware back to Klaus and patted him on the hand in forgiveness. 'You'll never be as nasty as Carmelita Spats,' she said.

'Carmelita Spats?' Violet said, lifting her head from her tray. She had dozed through Isadora and Klaus's argument but woken up at the sound of the Special Messenger's name. 'She's not

134

coming here again to tell us to do laps, is she?'

'I'm afraid she is,' Duncan said ruefully, a word which here means 'while pointing at a rude, violent, and filthy little girl.'

'Hello, cakesniffers,' Carmelita Spats said. 'Today I have two messages for you, so I should really get two tips instead of one.'

'Oh, Carmelita,' Klaus said. 'You haven't gotten a tip for the last nine days, and I see no reason to break that tradition.'

'That's because you're a stupid orphan,' Carmelita Spats said promptly. 'In any case, message number one is the usual: meet Coach Genghis on the front lawn right after dinner.'

Violet gave an exhausted groan. 'And what's the second message?' she asked.

'The second message is that you must report to Vice Principal Nero's office right away.'

'Vice Principal Nero's office?' Klaus asked. 'Why?'

'I'm sorry,' Carmelita Spats said with a nasty smile to indicate that she wasn't

135

sorry one bit. 'I don't answer questions from nontipping orphan cakesniffers.'

Some children at the neighboring table laughed when they heard that and began banging their silverware on the table. 'Cakesniffing orphans in the Orphans Shack! Cakesniffing orphans in the Orphans Shack!' they chanted as Carmelita Spats giggled and skipped off to finish her lunch. 'Cakesniffing orphans in the Orphans Shack! Cakesniffing orphans in the Orphans Shack!' they chanted while the Baudelaires sighed and stood up on their aching legs. 'We'd better go to Nero's,' Violet said. 'We'll see you later, Duncan and Isadora.'

'Nonsense,' Duncan said. 'We'll walk you. Carmelita Spats has made me lose my appetite, so we'll skip lunch and take you to the administrative building. We won't go inside—otherwise there'll be no silverware between the five of us—but we'll wait outside and you can tell us what's going on.'

'I wonder what Nero wants,' Klaus said, yawning.

'Maybe he's discovered that Genghis

is really Olaf, all by himself,' Isadora said, and the Baudelaires smiled back. They didn't dare hope that this was the reason for their summons to Nero's office, but they appreciated their friends' hopefulness. The five children handed their scarcely eaten lunches to the cafeteria workers, who blinked at them silently from behind their metal masks, and walked to the administrative building. The Quagmire triplets wished the Baudelaires luck, and Violet, Klaus, and Sunny trudged up the steps to Nero's office.

'Thank you for taking the time out of your busy orphan schedule to see me,' Vice Principal Nero said, yanking open his door before they could knock. 'Hurry up and come inside. Every minute I spend talking to you is a minute I could spend practicing the violin, and when you're a musical genius like me, every minute counts.'

The three children walked into the tiny office and began clapping their tired hands together as Nero raised both his arms in the air. 'There are two things I wanted to talk to you about,' he said when the applause was over. 'Do you know what they are?'

'No, sir,' Violet replied.

'*No, sir,*' Nero mimicked, although he looked disappointed that the children hadn't given him a longer answer to make fun of. 'Well, the first one is that the three of you have missed nine of my violin concerts, and each of you owes me a bag of candy for each one. Nine bags of candy times three equals twenty-nine. In addition, Carmelita Spats has told me that she has delivered ten messages to you, if you include the two she delivered today, and that you've never given her a tip. That's a disgrace. Now, I think a nice tip is a pair of earrings with precious stones, so you owe her ten pairs of earrings. What do you have to say about that?'

The Baudelaire orphans looked at one another with their sleepy, sleepy eyes. They had nothing to say about that. They had plenty to *think* about that—that they'd only missed Nero's concerts because Coach Genghis had forced them to, that nine bags of candy times three equals twenty-seven, not twenty-nine, and that tips are always optional and usually consist of money instead of earrings—but Violet, Klaus, and Sunny were too tired to say anything about it at all. This was another disappointment to Vice Principal Nero, who stood there scratching his pigtails and waiting for one of the children to say something that he could repeat in his nasty, mocking voice. But after a moment of silence, the vice principal went on to the second thing. 'The second thing,' he said, going on, 'is that you three have become the worst students Prufrock Preparatory School has ever seen. Violet, Mr. Remora tells me that you have flunked a test. Klaus, Mrs. Bass reports that you can scarcely tell one end of a metric ruler from another. And Sunny, I've noticed that you haven't made a single staple! Mr. Poe told me you were intelligent and hardworking children, but you're just a bunch of cakesniffers!'

At this, the Baudelaires could keep quiet no longer. 'We're flunking school because we're exhausted!' Violet cried.

'And we're exhausted because we're running laps every night!' Klaus cried.

'Galuka!' Sunny shrieked, which meant 'So yell at Coach Genghis, not at us!'

Vice Principal Nero gave the children a big smile, delighted that he was able to answer them in his favorite way. *'We're flunking school because we're exhausted!'* he squealed. *'And we're exhausted because we're running laps every night! Galuka!* I've had enough of your nonsense! Prufrock Preparatory School has promised you an excellent education, and an excellent education you will get—or, in Sunny's case, an excellent job as an administrative assistant! Now, I've instructed Mr. Remora and Mrs. Bass to give comprehensive exams tomorrow—large tests on absolutely everything you've learned so far. Violet, you'd better remember every detail of Mr. Remora's stories, and Klaus, you'd better remember the length, width, and depths of Mrs. Bass's objects, or I will expel you from school. Also, I've found a bunch of papers that need to be stapled tomorrow. Sunny, you will staple all of them, with homemade staples, or I will expel you from your job. First thing tomorrow morning we will have the test and the stapling, and if you don't get As and make enough staples, you'll leave Prufrock Preparatory School. Luckily for you, Coach Genghis has offered to homeschool you. That means he'd be your coach, your teacher, and your guardian, all in one. It's a very generous offer, and if I were you I'd give *him a* tip, too, although I don't think earrings are appropriate in this case.'

'We're not going to give Count Olaf a tip!' Violet blurted out.

Klaus looked at his older sister in horror. 'Violet means Coach Genghis,' Klaus said quickly to Nero.

'I *do not*!' Violet cried. 'Klaus, our situation is too desperate to pretend not to recognize him any longer!'

'Hifijoo!' Sunny agreed.

'I guess you're right,' Klaus said. 'What have we got to lose?'

141

'*What have we got to lose?*' Nero mocked. 'What are you talking about?'

'We're talking about Coach Genghis,' Violet said. 'He's not really named Genghis. He's not even a real coach. He's Count Olaf in disguise.'

'Nonsense!' Nero said.

Klaus wanted to say '*Nonsense!*' right back at Nero, in Nero's own repulsive way, but he bit his exhausted tongue. 'It's true,' he said. 'He's put a turban over his eyebrow and expensive running shoes over his tattoo, but he's still Count Olaf.'

'He has a turban for religious reasons,' Nero said, 'and running shoes because he's a coach. Look here.' He strode over to the computer and pressed a button. The screen began to glow in its usual seasick way, and once again showed a picture of Count Olaf. 'You see? Coach Genghis looks nothing like Count Olaf, and my advanced computer system proves it.'

'Ushilo!' Sunny cried, which meant 'That doesn't prove anything!'

'*Ushilo!*' Nero mocked. 'Who am I going to believe, an advanced computer system or two children flunking school and a little baby too dumb to make her own staples? Now, stop wasting my time! I will personally oversee tomorrow's comprehensive exams, which will be given in the Orphans Shack! And you'd better do excellent work, or it's a free ride from Coach Genghis! Sayonara, Baudelaires!'

'Sayonara' is the Japanese word for goodbye, and I'm sure that each and every one of the millions of people who live in Japan would be ashamed to hear their language used by such a revolting person. But the Baudelaire orphans had no time to think such international thoughts. They were too busy giving the Quagmire triplets the latest news.

'This is awful!' Duncan cried as the five children trudged across the lawn so they could talk things over in peace. 'There's no way you can get an A on those exams, particularly if you have to run laps tonight!'

'This is dreadful!' Isadora cried. 'There's no way you can make all those staples, either! You'll be homeschooled before you know it!'

'Coach Genghis won't homeschool us,' Violet said, looking out at the front lawn, where the luminous zero was waiting for them. 'He'll do something much, much worse. Don't you see? That's why he's made us run all those laps! He *knew* we'd be exhausted. He *knew* we'd flunk our classes, or fail to perform our secretarial duties. He *knew* we'd be expelled from Prufrock Prep, and then he could get his hands on us.'

Klaus groaned. 'We've been waiting for his plan to be made clear, and now it is. But it might be too late.'

'It's not too late,' Violet insisted. 'The comprehensive exams aren't until tomorrow morning. We must be able to figure out a plan by then.'

'Plan!' Sunny agreed.

'It'll have to be a complicated plan,' Duncan said. 'We have to get Violet ready for Mr. Remora's test, and Klaus ready for Mrs. Bass's test.'

'And we have to make staples,' Isadora said. 'And the Baudelaires still have to run laps.'

'And we have to stay awake,' Klaus said.

The children looked at one another, and then out at the front lawn. The afternoon sun was shining brightly, but the five youngsters knew that soon it would set behind the tombstone-shaped buildings, and that it would be time for S.O.R.E. They didn't have much time. Violet tied her hair up in a ribbon to keep it out of her eyes. Klaus polished his glasses and set them on his nose. Sunny scraped her teeth together, to make sure they were sharp enough for any task ahead. And the two triplets took their notebooks out of their sweater pockets. Coach Genghis's evil plan had become clear through the prism of the Baudelaire and Quagmire experiences, and now they had to use their experience to make a plan of their own.

CHAPTER TEN

The three Baudelaire orphans and the two Quagmire triplets sat in the Orphans Shack, which had never looked less unpleasant than it did now. All five children were wearing the noisy shoes Violet had invented, so the territorial crabs were nowhere to be seen. The salt had dried up the dripping tan fungus into a hard beige crust that was not particularly attractive but at least did not *plop!* drops of fungus juice on the youngsters. Because the arrival of Coach Genghis had focused their energies on defeating his treachery, the five orphans hadn't done anything about the green walls with the pink hearts on them, but otherwise the Orphans Shack had become quite a bit less mountainous and quite a bit more molehilly since the Baudelaires' arrival. It still had a long way to go to be attractive and comfortable living quarters, but for thinking of a plan, it would do in a pinch.

And the Baudelaire children were certainly in a pinch. If Violet, Klaus, and Sunny spent one more exhausting night running laps, they would flunk their comprehensive exams and secretarial assignment, and then Coach Genghis would whisk them away from Prufrock Prep, and as they thought of this they could almost feel Genghis's bony fingers pinching the life right out of them. The Quagmire triplets were so worried about their friends that they felt pinched as well, even though they were not directly in danger—or so they thought, anyway.

'I can't believe we didn't figure out Coach Genghis's plan earlier,' Isadora said mournfully, paging through her notebook. 'Duncan and I did all this research, and we still didn't figure it out.'

'Don't feel badly,' Klaus said. 'My sisters and I have had many encounters with Olaf, and it's always difficult to figure out his scheme.'

'We were trying to find out the history of Count Olaf,' Duncan said. 'The Prufrock Preparatory library has a pretty good collection of old newspapers, and we thought if we could find out some of his other schemes, we might figure out this one.'

'That's a good idea,' Klaus said thoughtfully. 'I've never tried that.'

'We figured that Olaf must have been an evil man even before he met you,' Duncan continued, 'so we looked up things in old newspapers. But it was difficult to find too many articles, because as you know he always uses a different name. But we found a person matching his description in the *Bangkok Gazette*, who was arrested for strangling a bishop but escaped from prison in just ten minutes.'

'That sounds like him, all right,' Klaus said.

'And then in the *Verona Daily News*,' Duncan said, 'there was a man who had thrown a rich widow off of a cliff. He had a tattoo of an eye on his ankle, but he had eluded authorities. And then we found a newspaper from your hometown that said—'

'I don't mean to interrupt,' Isadora said, 'but we'd better stop thinking about the past and start thinking about the present. Lunchtime is more than half over, and we desperately need a plan.'

'You're not napping, are you?' Klaus asked Violet, who had been silent for a very long time.

'Of course I'm not napping,' Violet replied. 'I'm concentrating. I think I can invent something to make all those staples Sunny needs. But I can't figure out how I can invent the device and study for the test at the same time. Since S.O.R.E. began, I haven't taken good notes in Mr. Remora's class, so I won't be able to remember his stories.'

'Well, you don't have to worry about that,' Duncan said, holding up his dark green notebook. 'I've written down every one of Mr. Remora's stories. Every boring detail is recorded here in my notebook.'

'And I've written down how long,

wide, and deep all of Mrs. Bass's objects are,' Isadora said, holding up her own notebook. 'You can study from my notebook, Klaus, and Violet can study from Duncan's.'

'Thank you,' Klaus said, 'but you're forgetting something. We're supposed to be running laps this evening. We don't have time to read anybody's notebook.'

'Tarcour,' Sunny said, which meant 'You're right, of course. S.O.R.E. always lasts until dawn, and the tests are first thing in the morning.'

'If only we had one of the world's great inventors to help us,' Violet said. 'I wonder what Nikola Tesla would do.'

'Or one of the world's great journalists,' Duncan said. 'I wonder what Dorothy Parker would do in this situation.'

'And I wonder what Hammurabi, the ancient Babylonian, would do to help us,' Klaus said. 'He was one of the world's greatest researchers.'

'Or the great poet Lord Byron,' Isadora said.

'Shark,' Sunny said, rubbing her

teeth thoughtfully.

'Who knows what any of those people or fish would do in our shoes?' Violet said. 'It's impossible to know.'

Duncan snapped his fingers, not to signal a waiter or because he was listening to catchy music but because he had an idea. 'In our shoes!' he said. 'That's it!'

'What's it?' Klaus asked. 'How will our noisy shoes help?'

'No, no,' Duncan said. 'Not the noisy shoes. I'm thinking about Coach Genghis's expensive running shoes that he said he couldn't take off because his feet were smelly.'

'And I bet they *are* smelly,' Isadora said. 'I've noticed he doesn't bathe much.'

'But that's not why he wears them,' Violet said. 'He wears them for a disguise.'

'Exactly!' Duncan said. 'When you said "in your shoes," it gave me an idea. I know you just meant "in our shoes" as an expression meaning "in our situation." But what if someone else were actually in your shoes—what if we disguised ourselves as you? Then we could run laps, and you could study for the comprehensive exams.'

'Disguise yourselves as us?' Klaus said. 'You two look exactly like each other, but you don't look anything like us.'

'So what?' Duncan said. 'It'll be dark tonight. When we've watched you from the archway, all we could see were two shadowy figures running—and one crawling.'

'That's true,' Isadora said. 'If I took the ribbon from your hair, Violet, and Duncan took Klaus's glasses, we'd look enough like you that I bet Coach Genghis couldn't tell.'

'And we could switch shoes, so your running on the grass would sound exactly the same,' Duncan said.

'But what about Sunny?' Violet asked. "There's no way two people could disguise themselves as three people.'

The Quagmire triplets' faces fell. 'If only Quigley were here,' Duncan said. 'I just know he'd be willing to dress up as a baby if it meant helping you.'

'What about a bag of flour?' Isadora asked. 'Sunny's only about as big as a bag of flour—nothing personal, Sunny.'

'Denada,' Sunny said, shrugging.

'We could snitch a bag from the cafeteria,' Isadora said, 'and drag it alongside us as we ran. From a distance, it would probably look enough like Sunny to avoid suspicion.'

'Being in each other's shoes seems like an extremely risky plan,' Violet said. 'If it fails, not only are we in trouble but you are as well, and who knows what Coach Genghis will do to you?'

This, as it turns out, was a question that would haunt the Baudelaires for quite some time, but the Quagmires gave it barely a thought. 'Don't worry about that,' Duncan said. 'The important thing is to keep you out of his clutches. It may be a risky plan, but being in each other's shoes is the only thing we've been able to think of.'

'And we don't have any time to waste thinking of anything else,' Isadora added. 'We'd better hurry if we want to snitch the bag of flour and not be late for class.'

'And we'll need a string, or something, so we can drag it along and make it look like Sunny crawling,' Duncan said.

'And I'll need to snitch some things, too,' Violet said, 'for my staple-making invention.'

'Nidop,' Sunny said, which meant something along the lines of 'Then let's get moving.'

The five children walked out of the Orphans Shack, taking off their noisy shoes and putting on their regular shoes so they wouldn't make a lot of noise as they walked nervously across the lawn to the cafeteria. They were nervous because they were not supposed to be sneaking into the cafeteria, or snitching things, and they were nervous because their plan was indeed a risky one. It is not a pleasant feeling, nervousness, and I would not wish for small children to be any more nervous than the Baudelaires and the Quagmires were as they walked toward the cafeteria in their regular shoes. But I must say that the children weren't nervous enough. They didn't need to be more nervous about sneaking into the cafeteria, even though it was against the rules, or snitching things, even though they didn't get caught. But they should have been more nervous about their plan, and about what would happen that evening when the sun set on the brown lawn and the luminous circle began to glow. They should have been nervous, now, in their regular shoes, about what would happen when they were in each other's.

CHAPTER ELEVEN

If you've ever dressed up for Halloween or attended a masquerade, you know that there is a certain thrill to wearing a disguise—a thrill that is half excitement and half danger. I once attended one of the famed masked balls hosted by the duchess of Winnipeg, and it was one of the most exciting and dangerous evenings of my life. I was disguised as a bullfighter and slipped into the party while being pursued by the palace guards, who were disguised as scorpions. The moment I entered the Grand Ballroom, I felt as if Lemony Snicket had disappeared. I was wearing clothes

I had never worn before—a scarlet cape made of silk and a vest embroidered with gold thread and a skinny black mask—and it made me feel as if I were a different person. And because I felt like a different person, I dared to approach a woman I had been forbidden to approach for the rest of my life. She was alone on the veranda—the word 'veranda' is a fancy term for a porch made of polished gray marble—and costumed as a dragonfly, with a glittering green mask and enormous silvery wings. As my pursuers scurried around the party, trying to guess which guest was me, I slipped out to the veranda and gave her the message I'd been trying to give her for fifteen long and lonely years. 'Beatrice,' I cried, just as the scorpions spotted me, 'Count Olaf is

I cannot go on. It makes me weep to think of that evening, and of the dark and desperate times that followed, and in the meantime I'm sure you are curious what happened to the Baudelaire orphans and the Quagmire triplets, after dinner that evening at Prufrock Prep.

'This is sort of exciting,' Duncan said, putting Klaus's glasses on his face. 'I know that we're doing this for serious reasons, but I'm excited anyway.'

Isadora recited, tying Violet's ribbon in her hair,

'It may not be particularly wise,
but it's a thrill to be disguised.'

'That's not a perfect poem, but it will have to do under the circumstances. How do we look?'

The Baudelaire orphans took a step back and regarded the Quagmires carefully. It was just after dinner, and the children were standing outside the Orphans Shack, hurriedly putting their risky plan into action. They had managed to sneak into the cafeteria and steal a Sunny-sized bag of flour from the kitchen while the metal-masked cafeteria workers' backs were turned. Violet had also snitched a fork, a few teaspoons of creamed spinach, and a small potato, all of which she needed for her invention. Now they had just a few moments before the Baudelaires—or, in this case, the Quagmires in disguise—had to show up for S.O.R.E. Duncan and Isadora handed over their notebooks so the Baudelaires could study for their comprehensive exams, and switched shoes so the Quagmires' laps would sound exactly like the Baudelaires'. Now, with only seconds to spare, the Baudelaires looked over the Quagmires' disguise and realized instantly just how risky this plan was.

Isadora and Duncan Quagmire simply did not look very much like Violet and Klaus Baudelaire. Duncan's eyes were of a different color from Klaus's, and Isadora had different hair from Violet's, even if it was tied up in a similar way. Being triplets, the Quagmires were the exact same height, but Violet was taller than Klaus because she was older, and there was no time to make small stilts for Isadora to mimic this height difference. But it wasn't really these small physical details that made the disguise so unconvincing. It was the simple fact that the Baudelaires and the Quagmires were different people, and a hair ribbon, a pair of glasses, and some shoes couldn't turn them into one another any more than a woman disguised as a dragonfly can actually take wing and escape the disaster awaiting her.

'I know we don't look much like you,' Duncan admitted after the Baudelaires had been quiet for some time. 'But remember, it's quite dark on the front lawn. The only light is coming from the luminous circle. We'll make sure to keep our heads down when we're running, so our faces won't give us away. We won't speak a word to Coach Genghis, so our voices won't give us away. And we have your hair ribbon, glasses, and shoes, so our accessories won't give us away, either.'

'We don't have to go through with this plan,' Violet said quietly. 'We appreciate your help, but we don't have to try and fool Genghis. My siblings and I could just run away right now, tonight. We've gotten to be pretty good runners, so we'd have a good head start on Coach Genghis.'

'We could call Mr. Poe from a pay phone somewhere,' Klaus said.

'Zubu,' Sunny said, which meant 'Or attend a different school, under different names.'

'Those plans don't have a chance of working,' Isadora said. 'From what you've told us about Mr. Poe, he's never very helpful. And Count Olaf seems to find you wherever you go, so a different school wouldn't help, either.'

'This is our only chance,' Duncan agreed. 'If you pass the exams without arousing Genghis's suspicion, you will be out of danger, and then we can focus our efforts on exposing the coach for who he really is.'

'I suppose you're right,' Violet said. 'I just don't like the idea of your putting your lives in such danger, just to help us.'

'What are friends for?' Isadora said. 'We're not going to attend some silly recital while you run laps to your

161

doom. You three were the first people at Prufrock Prep who weren't mean to us just for being orphans. None of us have any family, so we've got to stick together.'

'At least let us go with you to the front lawn,' Klaus said. 'We'll spy on you from the archway, and make sure you're fooling Coach Genghis.'

Duncan shook his head. 'You don't have time to spy on us,' he said. 'You have to make staples out of those metal rods and study for two comprehensive exams.'

'Oh!' Isadora said suddenly. 'How will we drag this bag of flour along the track? We need a string or something.'

'We could just kick it around the circle,' Duncan said.

'No, no, no,' Klaus said. 'If Coach Genghis thinks you're kicking your baby sister, he'll know something is up.'

'I know!' Violet said. She leaned forward and put her hand on Duncan's chest, running her fingers along his thick wool sweater until she found what she was looking for—a loose thread. Carefully, she pulled,

162

unraveling the sweater slightly until she had a good long piece of yarn. Then she snapped it off and tied one end around the bag of flour. The other end she handed to Duncan. 'This should do it,' she said. 'Sorry about your sweater.'

'I'm sure you can invent a sewing machine,' he said, 'when we're all out of danger. Well, we'd better go, Isadora. Coach Genghis will be waiting. Good luck with studying.'

'Good luck with running laps,' Klaus said.

The Baudelaires took a long look at their friends. They were reminded of the last time they saw their parents, waving good-bye to them as they left for the beach. They had not known, of course, that it would be the last moment they would spend with their mother and father, and again and again, each of the Baudelaires had gone back to that day in their lives, wishing that they had said something more than a casual good-bye. Violet, Klaus, and Sunny looked at the two triplets and hoped that this was not such a time, a time when people they

163

cared for would disappear from their lives forever. But what if it were?

'If we never see—' Violet stopped, swallowed, and began again. 'If something goes wrong—'

Duncan took Violet's hands and looked right at her. Violet saw, behind Klaus's glasses, the serious look in Duncan's wide eyes. 'Nothing will go wrong,' he said firmly, though of course he was wrong at that very moment. 'Nothing will go wrong at all. We'll see you in the morning, Baudelaires.'

Isadora nodded solemnly and followed her brother and the bag of flour away from the Orphans Shack. The Baudelaire orphans watched them walk toward the front lawn until the triplets were merely two specks, dragging another speck along with them.

'You know,' Klaus said, as they watched them, 'from a distance, in the dim light, they look quite a bit like us.'

'Abax,' Sunny agreed.

'I hope so,' Violet murmured. 'I hope so. But in the meantime, we'd better stop thinking about them and get started on our half of the plan. Let's put our noisy shoes on and go into the shack.'

'I can't imagine how you're going to make staples,' Klaus said, 'with only a fork, a few teaspoons of creamed spinach, and a small potato. That sounds more like the ingredients for a side dish than for a staple-making device. I hope your inventing skills haven't been dulled by a lack of sleep.'

'I don't think they have,' Violet said. 'It's amazing how much energy you can have once you have a plan. Besides, my plan doesn't only involve the things I snitched. It involves one of the Orphan Shack crabs and our noisy shoes. Now, when we all have our shoes on, please follow my instructions.'

The two younger Baudelaires were quite puzzled at this, but they had learned long ago that when it came to inventions, Violet could be trusted absolutely. In the recent past, she had invented a grappling hook, a lockpick, and a signaling device, and now, come hell or high water—an expression which here means 'using a fork, a few teaspoons of creamed spinach, a small potato, a live crab, and noisy shoes'—she was going to invent a staple-making device.

The three siblings put on their shoes and, following Violet's instructions, entered the shack. As usual, the tiny crabs were lounging around, taking advantage of their time alone in the shack when they wouldn't be frightened by loud noises. On most occasions, the Baudelaires would stomp wildly on the floor when they entered the shack, and the crabs would scurry underneath the bales of hay and into other hiding places in the room. This time, however, Violet instructed her siblings to step on the floor in carefully arranged patterns, so as to herd one of the grumpiest and biggest-clawed crabs into a corner of the shack. While the other crabs scattered, this crab was trapped in a corner, afraid of the noisy shoes but with nowhere to hide from them.

'Good work!' Violet cried. 'Keep him in the corner, Sunny, while I ready the potato.'

'What is the potato for?' Klaus asked.

'As we know,' Violet explained as Sunny tapped her little feet this way and that to keep the crab in the corner, 'these crabs love to get their claws on our toes. I specifically snitched a potato that was toe-shaped. You see how it's curved in a sort of oval way, and the little bumpy part here looks like a toenail?'

'You're right,' Klaus said. 'The resemblance is remarkable. But what does it have to do with staples?'

'Well, the metal rods that Nero gave us are very long, and need to be cut cleanly into small, staple-sized pieces. While Sunny keeps the crab in the corner, I'm going to wave the potato at him. He—or she, come to think of it, I don't know how to tell a boy crab from a girl crab—'

'It's a boy,' Klaus said. 'Trust me.'

'Well, he'll think it's a toe,' Violet continued, 'and snap at it with his claws. At that instant, I'll yank the potato away and put a rod in its place. If I do it carefully enough, the crab

167

should do a perfect job of slicing it up.'

'And then what?' Klaus asked.

'First things first,' Violet replied firmly. 'O.K. Sunny, keep tapping those noisy shoes. I'm ready with the potato and rod number one.'

'What can I do?' Klaus asked.

'You can start studying for the comprehensive exam, of course,' Violet said. 'I couldn't possibly read all of Duncan's notes in just one night. While Sunny and I make the staples, you need to read Duncan's and Isadora's notebooks, memorize the measurements from Mrs. Bass's class, and teach me all of Mr. Remora's stories.'

'Roger,' Klaus said. As you probably know, the middle Baudelaire was not referring to anybody named Roger. He was saying a man's name to indicate that he understood what Violet had said and would act accordingly, and over the course of the next two hours, that's exactly what he did. While Sunny used her noisy shoes to keep the crab in the corner and Violet used the potato as a toe and the crab's claws as clean cutters, Klaus used the Quagmire notebooks to study for the comprehensive exams, and everything worked the way it should. Sunny tapped her shoes so noisily that the crab remained trapped. Violet was so quick with the potato and metal rods that soon they were snipped into staple-sized pieces. And Klaus—although he had to squint because Duncan was using his glasses—read Isadora's measuring notes so carefully that before long he had memorized the length, width, and depth of just about everything.

'Violet, ask me the measurements of the navy blue scarf,' Klaus said, turning the notebook over so he couldn't peek.

Violet yanked the potato away just in time, and the crab snipped off another hit of the metal rods. 'What are the measurements of the navy blue scarf?' she asked.

'Two decimeters long,' Klaus recited, 'nine centimeters wide, and four millimeters thick. It's boring, but it's correct. Sunny, ask me the measurements of the bar of deodorant soap.'

The crab saw an opportunity to leave the corner, but Sunny was too quick for it. 'Soap?' Sunny quizzed Klaus, tapping her tiny noisy shoes until the crab retreated.

'Eight centimeters by eight centimeters by eight centimeters,' Klaus said promptly. 'That one's easy. You're doing great, you two. I bet that crab's going to be almost as tired as we are.'

'No,' Violet said, 'he's done. Let him go, Sunny. We have all the staple-sized pieces we need. I'm glad that part of the staple-making process is over. It's very nerve-wracking to tease a crab.'

'What's next?' Klaus said, as the crab scurried away from the most frightening moments of his life.

'Next you teach me Mr. Remora's stories,' Violet said, 'while Sunny and I bend these little bits of metal into the proper shape.'

'Shablo,' Sunny said, which meant something like 'How are we going to do that?'

'Watch,' Violet said, and Sunny watched. While Klaus closed Isadora's black notebook and began paging through Duncan's dark green one, Violet took the glob of creamed spinach and mixed it with a few pieces of stray hay and dust until it was a sticky, gluey mess. Then she placed this mess on the spiky end of the fork, and stuck it to one of the bales of hay so the handle end of the fork hung over the side. She blew on the creamed-spinach-stray-hay-and-dust mixture until it hardened. 'I always thought that Prufrock Prep's creamed spinach was awfully sticky,' Violet explained, 'and then I realized it could be used as glue. And now, we have a perfect method of making those tiny strips into staples. See, if I lay a strip across the handle of the fork, a tiny part of the strip hangs off each of the sides. Those are the parts that will go inside the paper when it's a staple. If I take off my noisy shoes'—and here Violet paused to take off her noisy shoes—'and use the metal ends to tap on the strips, they'll bend around the handle of the fork and turn into staples. See?'

'Gyba!' Sunny shrieked. She meant 'You're a genius! But what can I do to help?'

'You can keep your noisy shoes on your feet,' Violet replied, 'and keep the crabs away from us. And Klaus, you start summarizing stories.'

'Roger,' Sunny said.

'Roger,' Klaus said, and once again, neither of them were referring to Roger. They meant, once again, that they understood what Violet had said, and would act accordingly, and all three Baudelaires acted accordingly for the rest of the night. Violet tapped away at the metal strips, and Klaus read out loud from Duncan's notebook, and Sunny stomped her noisy shoes. Soon, the Baudelaires had a pile of homemade staples on the floor, the details of Mr. Remora's stories in their brains, and not a single crab bothering them in the shack, and even with the threat of Coach Genghis hovering over them, the evening actually began to feel rather cozy. It reminded the Baudelaires of evenings they had spent when their parents were alive, in one of the living rooms in the Baudelaire mansion. Violet would often be tinkering away at some invention, while Klaus would often be reading and sharing the information he was learning, and Sunny would often be making loud noises. Of course, Violet was never tinkering frantically at an invention that would save their lives, Klaus was never reading something so boring, and Sunny was never making loud noises to scare crabs, but nevertheless as the night wore on, the Baudelaires felt almost at home in the Orphans Shack. And when the sky began to lighten with the first rays of dawn, the Baudelaires began to feel a certain thrill that was quite different from the thrill of being in disguise. It was a thrill that I have never felt in my life, and it was a thrill that the Baudelaires did not feel very often. But as the morning sun began to shine, the Baudelaire orphans felt the thrill of thinking your plan might work after all, and that perhaps they would eventually be as safe and happy as the evenings they remembered.

CHAPTER TWELVE

Assumptions are dangerous things to make, and like all dangerous things to make—bombs, for instance, or strawberry shortcake—if you make even the tiniest mistake you can find yourself in terrible trouble. Making assumptions simply means believing things are a certain way with little or no evidence that shows you are correct, and you can see at once how this can lead to terrible trouble. For instance, one morning you might wake up and make the assumption that your bed was in the same place that it always was, even though you would have no real

evidence that this was so. But when you got out of your bed, you might discover that it had floated out to sea, and now you would be in terrible trouble all because of the incorrect assumption that you'd made. You can see that it is better not to make too many assumptions, particularly in the morning.

The morning of the comprehensive exams, however, the Baudelaire orphans were so tired, not only from staying up all night studying and making staples but also from nine consecutive nights of running laps, that they made plenty of assumptions, and every last one of them turned out to be incorrect.

'Well, that's the last staple,' Violet said, stretching her tired muscles. 'I think we can safely assume that Sunny won't lose her job.'

'And you seem to know every detail of Mr. Remora's stories as well as I know all of Mrs. Bass's measurements,' Klaus said, rubbing his tired eyes, 'so I think we can safely assume that we won't be expelled.'

'Nilikoh,' Sunny said, yawning her tired mouth. She meant something like 'And we haven't seen either of the Quagmire triplets, so I think we can safely assume that their part of the plan went well.'

'That's true,' Klaus said. 'I assume if they'd been caught we would have heard by now.'

'I'd make the same assumption,' Violet said.

'*I'd make the same assumption*,' came a nasty, mimicking voice, and the children were startled to see Vice Principal Nero standing behind them holding a huge stack of papers. In addition to the assumptions they had made out loud, the Baudelaires had made the assumption that they were alone, and they were surprised to find not only Vice Principal Nero but also Mr. Remora and Mrs. Bass waiting in the doorway of the Orphans Shack. 'I hope you've been studying all evening,' Nero said, 'because I told your teachers to make these exams extra-challenging, and the pieces of paper that the baby has to staple are very thick. Well, let's get started. Mr. Remora and Mrs. Bass will take turns asking you questions until one of you gets an answer wrong, and then you flunk. Sunny will sit in the back and staple these papers into booklets of five papers each, and if your homemade staples don't work perfectly, then *you* flunk. Well, a musical genius like myself doesn't have all day to oversee exams. I've missed too much practice time as it is. Let's begin!'

Nero threw the papers into a big heap on one of the bales of hay, and the stapler right after it. Sunny crawled over as quickly as she could and began inserting the staples into the stapler, and Klaus stood up, still clutching the Quagmire notebooks. Violet put her noisy shoes back on her feet, and Mr. Remora swallowed a bite of banana and asked his first question.

'In my story about the donkey,' he said, 'how many miles did the donkey run?'

'Six,' Violet said promptly.

'*Six*,' Nero mimicked. 'That can't be correct, can it, Mr. Remora?'

'Um, yes, actually,' Mr. Remora said, taking another bite of banana.

'How wide,' Mrs. Bass said to Klaus, 'was the book with the yellow cover?'

'Nineteen centimeters,' Klaus said immediately.

'*Nineteen centimeters*,' Nero mocked. 'That's wrong, isn't it, Mrs. Bass?'

'No,' Mrs. Bass admitted. 'That's the right answer.'

'Well, try another question, Mr. Remora,' Nero said.

'In my story about the mushroom,' Mr. Remora asked Violet, 'what was the name of the chef?'

'Maurice,' Violet answered.

'*Maurice*,' Nero mimicked.

'Correct,' Mr. Remora said.

'How long was chicken breast number seven?' Mrs. Bass asked.

'Fourteen centimeters and five millimeters,' Klaus said.

'*Fourteen centimeters and five millimeters*,' Nero mimicked.

'That's right,' Mrs. Bass said. 'You're actually both very good students, even if you've been sleeping through class lately.'

178

'Stop all this chitchat and flunk them,' Nero said. 'I've never gotten to expel any students, and I'm really looking forward to it.'

'In my story about the dump truck,' Mr. Remora said, as Sunny began to staple the pile of thick papers into booklets, 'what color were the rocks that it carried?'

'Gray and brown.'

'Gray and brown.'

'Correct.'

'How deep was my mother's casserole dish?'

'Six centimeters.'

'Six centimeters.'

'Correct.'

'In my story about the weasel, what was its favorite color?'

The comprehensive exams went on and on, and if I were to repeat all of the tiresome and pointless questions that Mr. Remora and Mrs. Bass asked, you might become so bored that you might go to sleep right here, using this book as a pillow instead of as an entertaining and instructive tale to benefit young minds. Indeed, the exams were so boring that the Baudelaire orphans might normally have dozed through the test themselves. But they dared not doze. One wrong answer or unstapled piece of paper, and Nero would expel them from Prufrock Preparatory School and send them into the waiting clutches of Coach Genghis, so the three children worked as hard as they could. Violet tried to remember each detail Klaus had taught her, Klaus tried to remember every measurement he had taught himself, and Sunny stapled like mad, a phrase which here means 'quickly and accurately.' Finally, Mr. Remora stopped in the middle of his eighth banana and turned to Vice Principal Nero.

'Nero,' he said, 'there's no use continuing these exams. Violet is a very fine student, and has obviously studied very hard.'

Mrs. Bass nodded her head in agreement. 'In all my years of teaching, I've never encountered a more metric-wise boy than Klaus, here. And it looks like Sunny is a fine secretary as well.

Look at these booklets! They're gorgeous.'

'Pilso!' Sunny shrieked.

'My sister means "Thank you very much," Violet said, although Sunny really meant something more like 'My stapling hand is sore.' 'Does this mean we get to stay at Prufrock Prep?'

'Oh, let them stay, Nero,' Mr. Remora said. 'Why don't you expel that Carmelita Spats? She never studies, and she's an awful person besides.'

'Oh yes,' Mrs. Bass said. 'Let's give *her* an extra-challenging examination.'

'I can't flunk Carmelita Spats,' Nero said impatiently. 'She's Coach Genghis's Special Messenger.'

'Who?' Mr. Remora asked.

'You know,' Mrs. Bass explained, 'Coach Genghis, the new gym teacher.'

'Oh yes,' Mr. Remora said. 'I've heard about him, but never met him. What is he like?'

'He's the finest gym teacher the world has ever seen,' Vice Principal Nero said, shaking his four pigtails in amazement. 'But you don't have to

181

take my word for it. You can see for yourself. Here he comes now.'

Nero pointed one of his hairy hands out of the Orphans Shack, and the Baudelaire orphans saw with horror that the vice principal was speaking the truth. Whistling an irritating tune to himself, Coach Genghis was walking straight toward them, and the children could see at once how incorrect one of their assumptions had been. It was not the assumption that Sunny would not lose her job, although that assumption, too, would turn out to be incorrect. And it was not the assumption that Violet and Klaus would not be expelled, although that, too, was a wrong one. It was the assumption about the Quagmire triplets and their part of the plan going well. As Coach Genghis walked closer and closer, the Baudelaires saw that he was holding Violet's hair ribbon in one of his scraggly hands and Klaus's glasses in the other, and with every step of his expensive running shoes, the coach raised a small white cloud, which the children realized must be flour from the snitched sack. But more than the ribbon, or the glasses, or the small clouds of flour was the look in Genghis's eyes. As Coach Genghis reached the Orphans Shack, his eyes were shining bright with triumph, as if he had finally won a game that he had been playing for a long, long time, and the Baudelaire orphans realized that the assumption about the Quagmire triplets had been very, very wrong indeed.

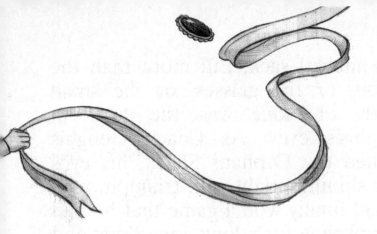

CHAPTER THIRTEEN

'Where are they?' Violet cried as Coach Genghis stepped into the shack. 'What have you done with them?' Normally, of course, one should begin conversations with something more along the lines of 'Hello, how are you,' but the eldest Baudelaire was far too distressed to do so.

Genghis's eyes were shining as brightly as could be, but his voice was calm and pleasant. 'Here they are,' he said, holding up the ribbon and glasses.

'I thought you might be worried about them, so I brought them over first thing in the morning.'

'We don't mean *these* them!' Klaus said, taking the items from Genghis's scraggly hands. 'We mean *them* them!'

'I'm afraid I don't understand all those thems,' Coach Genghis said, shrugging at the adults. 'The orphans ran laps last night as part of my S.O.R.E. program, but they had to dash off in the morning to take their exams. In their hurry, Violet dropped her ribbon and Klaus dropped his glasses. But the baby—'

'You know very well that's not what happened,' Violet interrupted. 'Where are the Quagmire triplets? What have you done with our friends?'

'*What have you done with our friends?*' Vice Principal Nero said in his mocking tone. 'Stop talking nonsense, orphans.'

'I'm afraid it's not nonsense,' Genghis said, shaking his turbaned head and continuing his story. 'As I was saying before the little girl interrupted me, the baby didn't dash off with the other orphans. She just sat there like a sack of flour. So I walked over to her and gave her a kick to get her moving.'

'Excellent idea!' Nero said. 'What a wonderful story this is! And then what happened?'

'Well, at first it seemed like I'd kicked a big hole in the baby,' Genghis said, his eyes shining, 'which seemed lucky, because Sunny was a terrible athlete and it would have been a blessing to put her out of her misery.'

Nero clapped his hands. 'I know just what you mean, Genghis,' he said. 'She's a terrible secretary as well.'

'But she did all that stapling,' Mr. Remora protested.

'Shut up and let the coach finish his story,' Nero said.

'But when I looked down,' Genghis continued, 'I saw that I hadn't kicked a hole in a baby. I'd kicked a hole in a bag of flour! I'd been tricked!'

'That's terrible!' Nero cried.

'So I ran after Violet and Klaus,' Genghis continued, 'and I found that they weren't Violet and Klaus after all, but those two other orphans—the twins.'

'They're not twins!' Violet cried. 'They're triplets!'

'*They're triplets!*' Nero mocked. 'Don't be an idiot. Triplets are when four babies are born at the same time, and there are only two Quagmires.'

'And these two Quagmires were pretending to be the Baudelaires, in order to give the Baudelaires extra time to study.'

'Extra time to study?' Nero said, grinning in delight. 'Hee hee hee! Why, that's cheating!'

'That's not cheating!' Mrs. Bass said.

'Skipping gym class to study is cheating,' Nero insisted.

'No, it's just good time management,' Mr. Remora argued. 'There's nothing wrong with athletics, but they shouldn't get in the way of your schoolwork.'

'Look, I'm the vice principal,' the vice principal said. 'I say the Baudelaires were cheating, and therefore—hooray!—I can expel them. You two are merely teachers, so if you disagree with me, I can expel you, too.'

Mr. Remora looked at Mrs. Bass,

and they both shrugged. 'You're the boss, Nero,' Mr. Remora said finally, taking another banana out of his pocket. 'If you say they're expelled, they're expelled.'

'Well, I say they're expelled,' Nero said. 'And Sunny loses her job, too.'

'Rantaw!' Sunny shrieked, which meant something along the lines of 'I never wanted to work as a secretary, anyway!'

'We don't care about being expelled,' Violet said. 'We want to know what happened to our friends.'

'Well, the Quagmires had to be punished for their part in the cheating,' Coach Genghis said, 'so I brought them over to the cafeteria and put those two workers in charge of them. They'll be whisking eggs all day long.'

'Very sensible,' Nero agreed.

'That's all they're doing?' Klaus said suspiciously. 'Whisking eggs?'

'That's what I said,' Genghis said and leaned so close to the Baudelaires that all they could see were his shiny eyes and the crooked curve of his wicked mouth. 'Those two Quagmires

188

will whisk and whisk until they are simply whisked away.'

'You're a liar,' Violet said.

'Insulting your coach,' Nero said, shaking his pigtailed head. 'Now you're doubly expelled.'

'What's this?' said a voice from the doorway. 'Doubly expelled?'

The voice stopped to have a long, wet cough, so the Baudelaires knew without looking that it was Mr. Poe. He was standing at the Orphans Shack holding a large paper sack and looking busy and confused. 'What are all of you doing here?' he said. 'This doesn't look like a proper place to have a conversation. It's just an old shack.'

'What are *you* doing here?' Nero asked. 'We don't allow strangers to wander around Prufrock Preparatory School.'

'Poe's the name,' Mr. Poe said, shaking Nero's hand. 'You must be Nero. We've talked on the phone. I received your telegram about the twenty-eight bags of candy and the ten pairs of earrings with precious stones. My associates at Mulctuary Money

Management thought I'd better deliver them in person, so here I am. But what's this about expelled?'

'These orphans you foisted on me,' Nero said, using a nasty word for 'gave,' 'have proven to be terrible cheaters, and I'm forced to expel them.'

'Cheaters?' Mr. Poe said, frowning at the three siblings. 'Violet, Klaus, Sunny, I'm very disappointed in you. You promised me that you'd be excellent students.'

'Well, actually, only Violet and Klaus were students,' Nero said. 'Sunny was an administrative assistant, but she was terrible at it as well.'

Mr. Poe's eyes widened in surprise as he paused to cough into his white handkerchief. 'An administrative assistant?' he repeated. 'Why, Sunny's only a baby. She should be in preschool, not an office environment.'

'Well, it doesn't matter now,' Nero said. 'They're all expelled. Give me that candy.'

Klaus looked down at his hands, which were still clutching the

Quagmire notebooks. He was afraid that the notebooks might be the only sign of the Quagmires he would ever see again. 'We don't have any time to argue about candy!' he cried. 'Count Olaf has done something terrible to our friends!'

'Count Olaf?' Mr. Poe said, handing Nero the paper sack. 'Don't tell me he's found you here!'

'No, of course not,' Nero said. 'My advanced computer system has kept him away, of course. But the children have this bizarre notion that Coach Genghis is actually Olaf in disguise.'

'Count Olaf,' Genghis said slowly. 'Yes, I've heard of him. He's supposed to be the best actor in the whole world. I'm the best gym teacher in the whole world, so we couldn't possibly be the same person.'

Mr. Poe looked Coach Genghis up and down, then shook his hand. 'A pleasure to meet you,' he said, and then turned to the Baudelaires. 'Children, I'm surprised at you. Even without an advanced computer system, you should be able to tell that this man isn't Count Olaf. Olaf has only one eyebrow, and this man is wearing a turban. And Olaf has a tattoo of an eye on his ankle, and this man is wearing expensive running shoes. They are quite handsome, by the way.'

'Oh, thank you,' Coach Genghis said. 'Unfortunately, thanks to these children, they have flour all over them, but I'm sure it'll wash off.'

'If he removes his turban and his shoes,' Violet said impatiently, 'you will be able to see that he's Olaf.'

'We've been through this before,' Nero said. 'He can't take off his running shoes because he's been exercising and his feet smell.'

'And I can't take off my turban for religious reasons,' Genghis added.

'You're not wearing a turban for religious reasons!' Klaus said in disgust, and Sunny shrieked something in agreement. 'You're wearing it as a disguise! Please, Mr. Poe, make him take it off!'

'Now, Klaus,' Mr. Poe said sternly. 'You have to learn to be accepting of other cultures. I'm sorry, Coach

Genghis. The children aren't usually prejudiced.'

'That's quite all right,' Genghis said. 'I'm used to religious persecution.'

'However,' Mr. Poe continued, after a brief coughing spell, 'I would ask you to remove your running shoes, if only to set the Baudelaires' minds at ease. I think we can all stand a little smelliness if it's in the cause of criminal justice.'

'Smelly feet,' Mrs. Bass said, wrinkling her nose. 'Ew, gross.'

'I'm afraid I cannot take off my running shoes,' Coach Genghis said, taking a step toward the door. 'I need them.'

'Need them?' Nero asked. 'For what?'

Coach Genghis took a long, long look at the three Baudelaires and smiled a terrible, toothy grin. 'For running, of course,' he said, and ran out the door.

The orphans were startled for a moment, not only because he had started running so suddenly but also because it seemed like he had given up so easily. After his long, elaborate plan—disguising himself as a gym teacher, forcing the Baudelaires to run laps, getting them expelled—he was suddenly racing across the lawn without even glancing back at the children he'd been chasing for such a long time. The Baudelaires stepped out of the Orphans Shack, and Coach Genghis turned back to sneer at them.

'Don't think I've given up on *you*, orphans!' he called to them. 'But in the meantime, I have two little prisoners with a very nice fortune of their own!'

He began to run again, but not before pointing a bony finger across the lawn. The Baudelaires gasped. At the far end of Prufrock Prep, they saw a long, black car with dark smoke billowing out of its exhaust pipes. But the children were not gasping at air pollution. The two cafeteria workers were walking toward the car, but they had taken off their metal masks at last, and the three youngsters could see that they were the two powder-faced women who were comrades of Count Olaf's. But this was not what the children were gasping at either, although it was a surprising and distressing turn of events. What they were gasping at was what each of the women was dragging toward the car. Each powder-faced woman was dragging one of the Quagmire triplets, who were struggling desperately to get away.

'Put them in the back seat!' Genghis called. 'I'll drive! Hurry!'

'What in the world is Coach Genghis doing with those children?' Mr. Poe asked, frowning.

The Baudelaires did not even turn to Mr. Poe to try and explain. After all their S.O.R.E. training sessions, Violet, Klaus, and Sunny found that their leg muscles could respond instantly if they wanted to run. And the Baudelaire orphans had never wanted to run more than they did now.

'After them!' Violet cried, and the children went after them. Violet ran, her hair flying wildly behind her. Klaus ran, not even bothering to drop the Quagmire notebooks. And Sunny crawled as fast as her legs and hands could carry her. Mr. Poe gave a startled cough and began running after them, and Nero, Mr. Remora, and Mrs. Bass began running after Mr. Poe. If you had been hiding behind the archway, spying on what was going on, you would have seen what looked like a strange race on the front lawn, with Coach Genghis running in front, the Baudelaire orphans right behind, and assorted adults huffing and puffing behind the children. But if you continued watching, you would have seen an exciting development in the race, a phrase which here means that the Baudelaires were gaining on Genghis. The coach had much longer legs than the Baudelaires, of course, but he had spent the last ten nights standing around blowing a whistle. The children had spent those nights running hundreds of laps around the luminous circle, and so their tiny, strong legs—and, in Sunny's case, arms —were overcoming Genghis's height advantage.

I hate to pause at such a suspenseful part of the story, but I feel I must intrude and give you one last warning as we reach the end of this miserable tale. You were probably thinking, as you read that the children were catching up to their enemy, that perhaps this was the time in the lives of the Baudelaire orphans when this terrible villain would finally be caught, and that perhaps the children would find some kind guardians and that Violet, Klaus, and Sunny would spend the rest of their lives in relative happiness, possibly creating the printing business that they had discussed with the Quagmires. And you are free to believe that this is how the story turns out, if you want. The last few events in this chapter of the Baudelaire orphans' lives are incredibly unfortunate, and quite terrifying, and so if you would prefer to ignore them entirely you should put this book down now and think of a gentle ending to this horrible story. I have made a solemn promise to write the Baudelaire history exactly as it occurred, but you have made no such promise—at least as far as I know—and you do not need to endure the wretched ending of this story, and this is your very last chance to save yourself from the woeful knowledge of what happened next.

Violet was the first to reach Coach Genghis, and she stretched her arm out as far as she could, grabbing part of his turban. Turbans, you probably know, consist of just one piece of cloth, wrapped very tightly and in a complicated way around someone's head. But Genghis had cheated, not knowing the proper way to tie a turban, because he was wearing it as a disguise and not for religious reasons. He had merely wrapped it around his head the way you might wrap a towel around yourself when getting out of the shower, so when Violet grabbed the turban, it unraveled immediately. She had been hoping that grabbing his turban would stop the coach from running, but all it did was leave her with a long piece of cloth in her hands. Coach Genghis kept running, his one eyebrow glistened with sweat over his shiny eyes.

'Look!' Mr. Poe said, who was far behind the Baudelaires but close enough to see. 'Genghis has only one eyebrow, like Count Olaf!'

Sunny was the next Baudelaire to reach Genghis, and because she was crawling on the ground, she was in a perfect position to attack his shoes. Using all four of her sharp teeth, she bit one pair of his shoelaces, and then the other. The knots came undone immediately, leaving tiny, bitten pieces of shoelace on the brown lawn. Sunny had been hoping that untying his shoes would make the coach trip, but Genghis merely stepped out of his shoes and kept running. Like many disgusting people, Coach Genghis was not wearing socks, so with each step his eye tattoo glistened with sweat on his left ankle.

'Look!' Mr. Poe said, who was still too far to help but close enough to see. 'Genghis has an eye tattoo, like Count Olaf! In fact, I think he is Count Olaf!'

'Of course he is!' Violet cried, holding up the unraveled turban.

'Merd!' Sunny shrieked, holding up a tiny piece of shoelace. She meant something like 'That's what we've been trying to tell you.'

Klaus, however, did not say anything. He was putting all of his energy toward running, but he was not running toward the man we can finally call by his true name, Count Olaf. Klaus was running toward the car. The powder-faced women were just shoving the Quagmires into the back seat, and he knew this might be his only chance to rescue them.

'Klaus! Klaus!' Isadora cried as he reached the car. Klaus dropped the notebooks to the ground and grabbed his friend's hand. 'Help us!'

'Hang on!' Klaus cried and began to drag Isadora back out of the car. Without a word, one of the powder-faced women leaned forward and bit Klaus's hand, forcing him to let go of the triplet. The other powder-faced woman leaned across Isadora's lap and began pulling the car door closed.

'No!' Klaus cried and grabbed the door handle. Back and forth, Klaus and Olaf's associate tugged on the door, forcing it halfway open and halfway shut.

'Klaus!' Duncan cried, from behind Isadora. 'Listen to me, Klaus! If anything goes wrong—'

'Nothing will go wrong,' Klaus promised, pulling on the car door as hard as he could. 'You'll be out of here in a second!'

'If anything goes wrong,' Duncan said again, 'there's something you should know. When we were researching the history of Count Olaf, we found out something dreadful!'

'We can talk about this later,' Klaus said, struggling with the door.

'Look in the notebooks!' Isadora cried. 'The—' The first powder-faced woman put her hand over Isadora's mouth so she couldn't speak. Isadora turned her head roughly and slipped from the woman's grasp. 'The—' The powdery hand covered her mouth again.

'Hang on!' Klaus called desperately. 'Hang on!'

'Look in the notebooks! V.F.D.' Duncan screamed, but the other woman's powdery hand covered his mouth before he could continue.

'What?' Klaus said.

Duncan shook his head vigorously and freed himself from the woman's hand for just one moment. 'V.F.D.' he managed to scream again, and that was the last Klaus heard. Count Olaf, who had been running slower without his shoes, had reached the car, and with a deafening roar, he grabbed Klaus's hand and pried it loose from the car door. As the door slammed shut, Olaf kicked Klaus in the stomach, sending him falling to the ground and landing with a rough *thump!* near the Quagmire notebooks he had dropped. The villain towered over Klaus and gave him a sickening smile, then leaned down, picked up the notebooks, and tucked them under his arm.

'No!' Klaus screamed, but Count Olaf merely smiled, stepped into the front seat, and began driving away just as Violet and Sunny reached their brother.

Clutching his stomach, Klaus stood up and tried to follow his sisters, who were trying to chase the long, black car. But Olaf was driving over the speed limit and it was simply impossible, and after a few yards the Baudelaires had to stop. The Quagmire triplets climbed over the powder-faced women and began to pound on the rear window of the car. Violet, Klaus, and Sunny could not hear what the Quagmires were screaming through the glass; they only saw their desperate and terrified faces. But then the powdery hands of Olaf's assistants grabbed them and pulled them back from the window. The faces of the Quagmire triplets faded to nothing, and the Baudelaires saw nothing more as the car pulled away.

'We have to go after them!' Violet screamed, her face streaked with tears. She turned around to face Nero and Mr. Poe, who were pausing for breath on the edge of the lawn. 'We have to go after them!'

'We'll call the police,' Mr. Poe gasped, wiping his sweaty forehead with his handkerchief. 'They have an advanced computer system, too. They'll catch him. Where's the nearest phone, Nero?'

'You can't use my phone, Poe!'

Nero said. 'You brought three terrible cheaters here, and now, thanks to you, my greatest gym teacher is gone and took two students with him! The Baudelaires are triple-expelled!'

'Now see here, Nero,' Poe said. 'Be reasonable.'

The Baudelaires sunk to the brown lawn, weeping with frustration and exhaustion. They paid no attention to the argument between Vice Principal Nero and Mr. Poe, because they knew, from the prism of their experience, that by the time the adults had decided on a course of action, Count Olaf would be long gone. This time, Olaf had not merely escaped but escaped with friends of theirs, and the Baudelaires wept as they thought they might never see the triplets again. They were wrong about this, but they had no way of knowing they were wrong, and just imagining what Count Olaf might do to their dear friends made them only weep harder. Violet wept, thinking of how kind the Quagmires had been to her and her siblings upon the Baudelaires' arrival at this dreadful academy. Klaus wept, thinking of how the Quagmires had risked their lives to help him and his sisters escape from Olaf's clutches. And Sunny wept, thinking of the research the Quagmires had done, and the information they hadn't had time to share with her and her siblings.

The Baudelaire orphans hung on to one another, and wept and wept while the adults argued endlessly behind them. Finally—as, I'm sorry to say, Count Olaf forced the Quagmires into puppy costumes so he could sneak them onto the airplane without anyone noticing—the Baudelaires cried themselves out and just sat on the lawn together in weary silence. They looked up at the smooth gray stone of the tombstone buildings and at the arch with 'PRUFROCK PREPARATORY SCHOOL' in enormous black letters and the motto 'Memento Mori' printed beneath. They looked out at the edge of the lawn, where Olaf had snatched the Quagmire notebooks. And they took long, long looks at one another. The Baudelaires remembered, as I'm sure you remembered, that in times of extreme stress one can find energy hidden in even the most exhausted areas of the body, and Violet, Klaus, and Sunny felt that energy surge through them now.

'What did Duncan shout to you?' Violet asked. 'What did he shout to you from the car, about what was in the notebooks?'

'V.F.D.' Klaus said, 'but I don't know what it means.'

'Ceju,' Sunny said, which meant 'We have to find out.'

The older Baudelaires looked at their sister and nodded. Sunny was right. The children had to find out the secret of V.F.D. and the dreadful thing the Quagmires had discovered. Perhaps it could help them rescue the two triplets. Perhaps it could bring Count Olaf to justice. And perhaps it could somehow make clear the mysterious and deadly way that their lives had become so unfortunate.

A morning breeze blew through the campus of Prufrock Preparatory School, rustling the brown lawn and knocking against the stone arch with the motto printed on it. 'Memento Mori'—'Remember you will die.' The Baudelaire orphans looked up at the motto and vowed that before they died, they would solve this dark and complicated mystery that cast a shadow over their lives.

LEMONY SNICKET first received his

education from public schools and private tutors, and then vice versa. He has been hailed as a brilliant scholar, discredited as a brilliant fraud, and mistaken for a much taller man on several occasions. Mr. Snicket's researching skills are currently and devoutly concentrated on the plight of the Baudelaire orphans, published serially by Egmont Books. Email to lemony.snicket@ecb.egmont.com

BRETT HELQUIST was born in Ganado, Arizona, grew up in Orem, Utah, and now lives in New York City. He earned a bachelor's degree in fine arts from Brigham Young University and has been illustrating ever since. His art has appeared in many publications, including *Cricket* magazine and *The New York Times.*

To My Kind Editor,

Please excuse this ridiculously fancy stationery. I am writing to you from 667 Dark Avenue, and this is the only paper available in the neighborhood. My investigation of the Baudelaire orphans' stay in this wealthy and woeful place is finally complete—I only pray that the manuscript will reach you.

Not next Tuesday, but the Tuesday after that, purchase a first-class, one-way ticket on the second-to-last train out of the city. Instead of boarding the train, wait until it departs and climb down to the tracks to retrieve the complete

summary of my
investigation, entitled
THE ERSATZ ELEVATOR, as
well as one of Jerome's
neckties, a small
photograph of Veblen
Hall, a bottle of parsley
soda, and the doorman's
coat, so that Mr.
Helquist can properly
illustrate, this terrible
chapter in the
Baudelaires' lives.
  Remember, you are my
last hope that the tales
of the Baudelaire orphans
can finally be told to
the general public.

With all due respect,

Lemony Snicket

Lemony Snicket